RISE UP

RISE UP

ALISON BROWNSTONE™ BOOK TWELVE

JUDITH BERENS   MARTHA CARR   MICHAEL ANDERLE

DISRUPTIVE IMAGINATION®

Copyright © 2019 Judith Berens, Martha Carr and Michael Anderle
Cover by Fantasy Book Design
Cover copyright © LMBPN Publishing
A Michael Anderle Production

LMBPN Publishing
PMB 196, 2540 South Maryland Pkwy
Las Vegas, NV 89109

First US edition, August 2019
Version 1.01, August 2019
Print ISBN: 978-1-64202-797-6

THE RISE UP TEAM

Thanks to the JIT Readers

Shari Regan
Daniel Weigert
Peter Manis
Diane L. Smith
Dave Hicks
Dorothy Lloyd
Nicole Emens
Paul Westman
Jeff Eaton
John Ashmore

If we've missed anyone, please let us know!

Editor
SkyHunter Editing Team

DEDICATIONS

From Martha

To everyone who still believes in magic
and all the possibilities that holds.
To all the readers who make this
entire ride so much fun.
And to my son, Louie and so many wonderful friends who
remind me all the time of what
really matters and how wonderful
life can be in any given moment.

From Michael

To Family, Friends and
Those Who Love
To Read.
May We All Enjoy Grace
To Live The Life We Are
Called.

CHAPTER ONE

Alison gritted her teeth and poured more magic into her wings. She needed more speed. A shadow blast struck a tree and severed a branch, but a quick turn saved her from the falling wood. Magic swelled behind her, and she dove toward the ground. The source of the magic, a dark purple beam, missed her by seconds and tunneled through a tree trunk.

That was close. Too close.

"Hey," she shouted and amplified her voice with the help of a hasty spell. "A few downed branches here and there is one thing, but don't cut trees down." She looked over her shoulder and frowned.

Two shadow-winged Drow women soared through the forest and twisted and turned between the trees—Rasila and Miar. The latter gripped her sword in her hand, the source of the previous beam. Unlike Alison's preferred shadowy choice, this weapon was an actual physical object.

This is supposed to be some friendly training, not a logging trip.

"Oh, don't worry, Alison," Rasila called in response with a little too much glee in her voice. "We'll fix any serious damage once we're finished. But if we don't try hard, this little training exercise is pointless."

Alison lowered altitude and released her wings. She tucked into a roll and her layers of shields took the force of the impact. As a follow-through, she bounded to her feet and raised her palms to quickly fire several bright bolts of light magic. There might be two Drow princesses after her, but that didn't mean she needed to give up.

Her attacks struck the shadow nimbuses that surrounded Rasila and Miar. The women altered course to circle her on either side while they replied with rapid flurries of shadow orbs and a few sharp shadow crescents. She dashed forward and the magic reduced the earth behind her to dirt, wood splinters, and shredded undergrowth like green confetti. She resisted the urge to duck behind a tree, fearing another impromptu lumberjack session.

One of Rasila's shadow orbs exploded against her shield. She staggered but felt only a light sting. Her phone chimed infuriatingly as she spun toward her opponent and prepared to launch a counterattack.

"Oh, crap," she muttered and raised a palm to indicate time out.

The two princesses stopped their swoops and hovered in place to watch her with confused expressions after they exchanged a befuddled glance.

Alison groaned. "Sorry. I totally forgot about a meeting I had today. It was an impromptu thing that came up a few days ago, and I don't coordinate my Drow...uh, time with my personal assistant." She released the magic that fueled her defenses and wiped the sweat off her forehead. "But that was a good workout. Thanks, both of you."

The Drow ceased fueling their wings and floated down beside her. Rasila smirked but Miar frowned.

"You continue to impress, Alison," Rasila commented and her smirk turned into a smile. "Most couldn't hold off two Drow princesses with so little damage. Your natural instincts serve you well."

"You weren't going all out," she replied.

Miar sheathed her sword. "Neither were you. I'm well aware of the level of destruction you can wreak when you're so inclined."

"It's not like we were actually trying to kill each other." Alison gestured to the sword. "I've never asked about that. Why do you use an actual sword instead of a shadow blade? I understand that it's an artifact, but is it really that much better?"

The princess glanced at her sword. "Better is a relative consideration. The sword can help me with my shadow compression so I can accomplish, as you've seen, certain types of attacks more quickly and with more power. But it's also far more limited in the types of shadow magic it can accomplish, let alone general spells." She patted the hilt. "As for why I use it, I've become accustomed to it. It helped me defeat a dangerous creature when I was younger and my magic far less refined. It's a useful reminder."

"Of what?"

Miar stared into the trees for a few seconds. "That even the smallest advantage can save you in a battle."

It sounds like an interesting story, but she doesn't really look like she wants to tell it.

Rasila scoffed. "You merely like the idea of wandering around with a sword, but at least you didn't wear the armor today."

"I assume it's also magical?" Alison asked.

Miar nodded her confirmation. "Even if there are few opportunities for true battle among the Drow, there are still many dangerous creatures on Oriceran. Hunting them when they threaten others has provided me with numerous opportunities to strengthen my skills throughout the decades. Perhaps someday, we can hunt such creatures together."

Alison raised a hand. "I remember hearing a little about that when I was over there, but I have more than enough nonsense here to keep me busy."

Rasila cleared her throat. "Since we're discussing Oriceran and Drow matters more in general, I do feel I should share a piece of information with both of you that has recently come to my attention."

The other two women turned toward her, curiosity in their eyes.

"Novati and Drae are aware that we're in contact," she explained. "You might not understand this, Alison, given your rather human way of looking at time, but our regular meetings would be considered unusually often by Drow standards and even all three of us meeting after a month could be considered the same. There are a few implications to that."

Miar shrugged. "Was this supposed to be some grand secret? I've been open about my contact with both you and Alison. I have no desire to sneak around in the shadows and plot, but I'm not worried about them."

"Oh?" Alison folded her arms over her chest. "That's fairly blasé, considering everything that's going on. I appreciate you two training with me, but if they view it as an alliance, they might decide to target us in a big way." She frowned. "Maybe I should reach out to them to make my position clear. The last thing I need is a Drow princess attacking me." She glared at Rasila. "It wastes my time."

Rasila wrinkled her nose. "Novati is like Miar without any of the charm or honor, and Drae is duplicitous. Perhaps you should be cautious, Alison."

"Meaning what?" She looked from one to the other and sighed. "Should I be worried about assassination attempts?"

Miar furrowed her brow. "I can't dispute Rasila's characterizations, even if I would not describe them in such a manner, but you have no reason to fear assassination attempts." She frowned at the other Drow. "Only ridiculous schemes that might challenge you."

Rasila offered a bright smile in response. "I suppose that's true enough on both counts. Caution is still warranted."

"Are you sure?" Alison asked. "I have so many things going on. If they intend to attack me or even challenge me in some way, I need to know so I can prepare and let my people know."

If any Drow princess hurt any of her friends or employees, Alison would demonstrate to them exactly how much like her father she could be.

Miar shook her head. "Novati might challenge you at some point, but it will be open and direct. She won't resort to assassination. Drae wouldn't even dare. They might have their flaws, but they are still Drow princesses and Drow royalty will not kill other Drow royalty." She scowled. "Even most Drow wouldn't dare. For all their claims of her wickedness, Laena remains a prisoner."

Alison sighed. She'd been vaguely aware of that when she traveled to Oriceran to train with the Drow, but everyone avoided the subject of the deposed queen, another victim on the long list of people who shouldn't have pissed her father off.

She could have left us alone, but she sent assassins and even managed to set the Light Elves against us, even before her little final stunt in court. She had so many chances to walk away but she refused. Some people only learn the hard way.

"I think your diplomatic instincts are the correct ones," Miar explained. "It's why I spend time with both you and Rasila. I think that if all five princesses deal with each other in a straight-forward and honorable fashion, we can come to some kind of agreement. I've tried speaking to Novati and Drae, but they've been far less receptive to my overtures."

Rasila snorted. "I don't know if that's admirable or naïve. Perhaps both. For the oldest among us, you cling to some outdated notions. For your sake, I hope they don't take advantage of you."

"Not trying to piss other Drow princesses off isn't a bad idea." Alison frowned. "But I thought of something. Laena's still alive, right? At least she was the last time I heard."

Rasila nodded. "The execution of the queen wouldn't be something that would escape my notice—or any Drow's, for that matter."

"We can't execute the queen," Miar insisted with a

decisive sweep of her hand. "Even if she might deserve it, such an action would plunge the Drow into true civil war. She still has her supporters, even though the Guardians are keeping things under control for the moment."

Rasila sneered. "And only barely. Pro-Laena forces have committed acts of terrorism that risk turning the eye of King Oriceran on the Drow, and the last thing we need is the Light Elves involving themselves in an internal matter. That is all the more reason to establish a firm new queen as quickly as possible. What was taken from Laena can be returned, and if she does regain power, I suspect the traitorous princesses who didn't agitate for her return will be punished."

Alison waved her hands in protest. "To be clear, I'm not asking for her to be executed. I was merely curious, but now that you've said all that, what about Novati and Drae? Do they support the queen?"

"Perhaps," Miar admitted and looked troubled. "But if they do, they've not stated it publicly. Drae wouldn't surprise me, but I find it hard to believe a boastful and arrogant woman such as Novati would hide her intentions. She always did admire Laena's ruthlessness and has often emulated it."

Alison sighed. "I think we all can agree that these are unusual times for the Drow and we should all be a little more careful. Miar, you keep saying that princesses will never harm princesses, but for hundreds of years, no one would have thought the Drow would turn against their queen like that either. Maybe you shouldn't be so sure."

Miar scoffed. "Let either Drae or Novati attack me. If

they do, they'll be lucky if they escape with their lives." She crushed a pinecone under her boot heel in annoyance.

I'm not sure if that's confidence or arrogance.

Rasila tapped her bottom lip. "I can't say I disagree with your analysis, but I'm far less concerned about them assassinating any of us versus undermining our political position—particularly yours, Alison, given your refusal to vie for the position."

Alison shrugged. "I only want what's best for the Drow, and I don't think that's me as queen."

"Perhaps."

Her phone chimed again. "I need to get back to my office."

Miar raised her hands and chanted a spell. A swirling portal appeared.

"That's still one trick that's beyond me." Alison pointed to the portal. "There's all the proof you need that I don't deserve to be queen."

Rasila shook her head. "I refuse to believe it's beyond you given your current power, but that's something else we can discuss in the future. Reach out to the others if you desire, Alison, but keep in mind you have one ally already." She glanced at Miar. "And at least one other woman you know won't stab you in the back."

Miar nodded, a serious look on her face.

"Take care of the trees you damaged." She stepped through the portal into the lobby of the Brownstone Building.

Ava stood beside the receptionist desk, her arms folded and a look of faint annoyance on her face. "You didn't tell me you were going to go off with Drow today, Miss Brownstone."

"It was kind of a last-minute thing," she explained with a sheepish grin. "You know how it goes. Three princesses call each other and try to get their schedules to match up."

Ava sighed and lowered her arms. "Let's get to your meeting, and you have your little personal errand afterward."

Her face heated. "I know. You don't...need to keep track of that kind of thing for me."

"I don't need to, but it might be helpful."

"Don't I have a meeting to go to?" Alison asked and avoided looking at the other woman.

CHAPTER TWO

Her expression scrunched in concentration, Alison's gaze roved over the glass cases at the jewelry store that displayed a variety of rings, pendants, and necklaces encrusted with diamonds, rubies, and emeralds. A few other gems adorned pieces here and there, including more exotic options most likely from Oriceran. One ring glowed a constant dull purple, but she didn't sense any magic from it. Another array of tiny gems shifted colors slowly as the minutes passed.

Mason scratched his cheek and gestured to a nearby case. "It's your choice, A. I've never been much of a jewelry man, and I know you won't demand something expensive for the sake of being expensive."

She leaned over a display to peer more closely at a simple band with a single solitaire diamond. "Maybe I should start."

"Start what?" Mason asked.

"Being expensive for the sake of being expensive." She gave him a challenging look.

He grinned. "That might be interesting, but I think it's a little too late now."

The owner of the shop—a middle-aged woman with graying hair and a plastic smile—stood in the corner and watched without comment. She had expressed earlier excitement at the idea of Alison Brownstone's wedding ring being purchased from her shop but hadn't pressured them at all. Alison appreciated that. There was nothing more annoying than a hard sell.

She frowned and straightened. "Do you think we should be further along?"

"Huh?" He shook his head. "I don't understand."

"With the wedding planning," she clarified. "It's been a month since your proposal, and we don't have anything worked out."

Mason shrugged. "I've never gotten married before, but I don't think there's a particular schedule."

"That's true. My dad took forever to even come up with a proposal, and the wedding took a while after that." She stared at another ring that featured a prominent black opal.

Maybe something non-traditional? I'm a non-traditional woman from a non-traditional family.

Alison grimaced at another intrusive thought. "There isn't a ring from your grandmother or something I'm supposed to use, is there? I know I'm not your parents' first choice in daughters-in-law, though."

He laughed. "No, nothing like that. My family might be very obsessed with the tradition of being healers, but they aren't nearly as bad with other traditions. We can decide what we want for our own wedding, and they won't complain as long as they're invited."

She stared at him. "And if we chose to elope?"

His smile fell but he nodded slowly. "I have your back, A. I always will. I won't lie and say there wouldn't be certain practical advantages to that, even if there would be complaints. I could handle my family. What about yours?"

"My dad wouldn't care unless he thought he was missing a chance at barbecue." Alison scowled. "And I won't have barbecue at my wedding anyway, no matter what. I should have sushi simply to mess with him."

Mason laughed. "That's fine by me. The truth is, I don't care that much about the details as long as you're happy. I have the yes from you, and that's what I care about. If you want to elope, that's no problem. If you want to bridezilla this, we can do that, too."

Alison rolled her eyes. "I definitely will not turn into a bridezilla." Her gaze returned to the display cases. "But it might help if I could at least decide what kind of ring I want." She pointed to an unadorned band with a small square-cut diamond. "Maybe something like this."

He stared at the ring for a moment and a flicker of confusion crossed his face. "Really?"

"Why? What's wrong with it?"

"Nothing. But it's very simple. It's actually smaller than the engagement ring." He shrugged. "I won't complain. My bank account would thank you, and I wouldn't have to ask my hot boss for a raise." He winked.

She laughed. "I don't ever want to take it off. If it's simple and not too fancy, I don't have to worry about it on jobs and when I'm out there kicking ass. That's my thought here."

"Fair enough. Like I said, whatever you want is fine by me."

The door sensor chimed as two men in ski masks threw the door open. Both held wands.

You have to be kidding me.

The owner yelped in surprise. "I don't want any trouble," she shouted and raised her hands. "Especially magical trouble."

One of the men smiled. "Good," he replied in a gravelly voice. "Then you and dye job and her boyfriend need to get over here and lay down on the ground with your hands on your head. If you all do that, no one gets hurt. If not...well, you get to see the power of magic up close."

The owner swallowed. A pleading look entered her eyes, but she walked slowly around the counter, her hands still raised.

Alison scoffed and pointed to her white hair. "I suppose I'm dye job?"

"Dyeing your hair to stand out, sweet cakes?" The robber snorted. "I'm not saying you don't have a little something going on. I like my chicks athletic, but the hair is too needy." He pointed his wand at the floor. "And I'd hate to mess up a face like that. So get down."

Mason glared at him. "I'll deal with the two of you first."

The robber laughed and pointed his wand at the life wizard. "This isn't the time to try to look tough in front of your girl, cowboy."

The owner completed her retreat around the counter. She lay on the floor and placed her hands on her head.

Alison sighed. "You really have no idea who I am, do you?"

The robbers exchanged looks and the first one shrugged. "Who are you supposed to be?"

"I'm Alison Brownstone."

The man who'd done all the talking snorted. "And I'm James Brownstone. Get down, bitch, before I decide to take more than diamonds."

She stepped in front of Mason and summoned a shield with a quick movement of her arm. Mason yanked his wand out of the concealed holster under his jacket in one fluid motion and rattled off an incantation for his own shield spell so quickly she could barely understand him.

The two robbers leapt back, their wands at the ready, and their eyes widened.

Alison summoned a shadow blade. "This is your one chance to surrender. Don't feel too bad. You're merely very, very unlucky."

The first robber growled. "You're not Alison Brownstone. Just because you have a few tricks don't mean shit."

She brandished the shadow blade. "I cast a shield spell and summoned this shadow blade without an incantation, didn't I?"

"A," Mason muttered, "Don't do anything rash. Remember what I said?"

"Sure. Don't worry." She turned her head to look at the second robber. "I'll let you have the first guy."

The accomplice frowned and took a few more steps back until he was almost against the wall. He flashed the first man a questioning look.

"Now, what'll it be?" Alison asked. "We were in the middle of something when you showed up."

The wizards both screamed their incantations. She launched herself forward as fireballs erupted from their wands and slammed into her shield. Her defenses held but she hissed at the impact.

At the last moment, she rushed toward the flank of the second man and released her shadow blade. He turned and delivered another fireball at point-blank range. Her shield weakened, the spell now barely visible. A stun spell extended from her hand as a blue-white rod of energy.

The first robber's eyes continue to track her, and he began a rapid chant for another spell—a restraining spell from the sound of it. His tactical mistake became obvious a moment later when Mason pounded a glowing fist into his head. The criminal spun a few times before he sagged and fell with a dull thud, unconscious.

These arrogant idiots didn't even use shields.

The man's partner jerked his wand to point at the cowering store owner. "Back off," he warned. "You might be able to take it, but can she?"

Mason grunted and kicked the wand away from the downed wizard. He glared at the remaining criminal but said nothing.

Alison raised her stun rod. "Do you really want to do this? Do you really want to harm an innocent woman?"

"Some rich bitch who owns a jewelry store?" The man scoffed. "I'll be able to live with myself."

"You have magic. There are so many ways you could make money even with the difficulties of directly conjuring something valuable." She shook her head. "You can't justify this robbery because she has something you don't when you have a fundamentally more special ability."

His grin widened. "It doesn't matter. All that matters is that I'll take that woman as my hostage and we'll take a little trip. Once I'm far enough away, I'll let her go. But if you try anything, she gets it." He licked his lips. "And I'll take a few of the pieces here for my trouble."

"Do what you need to, A," Mason intoned. "I have your back."

Alison sighed. "I had to give him his chance." She sprinted forward.

Mason threw himself over the shop owner.

The wizard growled but he didn't manage a single syllable before she shoved her summoned stun rod into his chest. His eyes rolled toward the back of his head, and a pained moan escaped his lips before he dropped and twitched on the floor.

She knelt beside him, released the stun rod, and held the man's hands together before she muttered a spell. A small length of rope appeared, and she bound his hands.

Mason stood and conjured a second rope to tie up the other man.

The shop owner sat slowly and put a hand to her chest, breathing erratically. "Thank you. I have insurance, but it wouldn't have covered all my losses if they cleaned my shop out." She stood and pointed to the ring Alison had been considering before they'd been interrupted. "I'd like to give it to you as a gift and as my way of saying thanks."

Alison shook her head. "That's okay."

"Please, no, I insist." The woman smiled. "Not only did

you stop these men, but you stopped them without damaging my shop, and well…" Her smile turned sheepish.

"Well, what?"

Mason smirked. "You do have a reputation, A. Not many people in Seattle are single-handedly responsible for a bridge closure. Just saying."

She groaned. "I was stopping a Mountain Strider at the time." She scrubbed a hand down her face. "I'll take the ring. We can size it while we wait for the cops to arrive."

CHAPTER THREE

Alison leaned back on her couch, her phone to her ear. Raucous laughter erupted from the other side.

"It's not that funny, Izzie," she complained.

"Yes, it is," her friend countered. "It's like the universe loves to mess with you. With both of us." Her voice turned serious. "Is this line secure?"

"Not totally."

The defeat of the Seventh Order meant Izzie could come out of hiding, and they no longer had to rely on self-destructing magical notes and the brief occasional meeting. The friends might not talk as often as Alison would have liked, but it was still wonderful to be able to communicate like two normal people and not like spies afraid of being executed, even if they both still needed the occasional precaution. Despite all that, she didn't enjoy her friend laughing at her.

Izzie snickered. "Well, let's say your dad had his fun during his proposal and all his wedding prep misadventures, and now, you've inherited the messed-up Brownstone tradition. You can't even go ring shopping without trouble. That's at least a little funny. And I've been on several dates now with Luke and nothing bad has happened, but the minute you go out to dinner with him, dark wizard assassins suddenly show up."

She scoffed. "Now you're saying I'm bad l— Wait a second."

Did she say what I think she said?

Her friend laughed again. "I'm not saying you're bad luck. I'm only saying trouble happens around you. I get it. I used to have the same problem, although it seems like the universe is cutting me a break now that the Seventh Order garbage is over. So the Berens luck is good now, and the Brownstone situation is different."

"Slow down," Alison insisted. "You're passing over the most important part of this."

"You can't be mad because I'm taking it slow for a while and crazy conspiracies aren't popping up around me. Don't worry. I'm sure I'll take a trip and end up knee-deep in a weird magical mystery."

Is she messing with me now?

Alison coughed. "I'm not talking about that. I'm talking about the part where you went on several dates with Luke. The last time we discussed him for more than thirty seconds, you said you had seen him a couple of times and didn't really think it was going anywhere, that kind of thing. It definitely didn't seem like you were ready to date him regularly."

Izzie laughed. It approached a nervous titter, which seemed wrong coming from her. "You know what they say. No plan survives contact with the ex-boyfriend."

"Who says that?"

"You know, people. Or at least some smart-mouthed pixie somewhere."

She straightened and her heart rate kicked up. "Spill. I didn't think anything you said before about not being the same girl was crazy, but I won't exactly be sad if you and Luke get back together. He's grown into a good man, and it wasn't like he was a bad boy."

The other woman released a long, wistful sigh. "And he's not bad to look at, either. He's certainly filled out even more than before."

Alison glanced around. Mason was still upstairs, and Sonya remained sequestered in her room slash de facto cave lair. "Yeah, I won't claim he isn't nice to look at. That's a bonus along with him actually caring about helping other people, bravery, and all those other nice qualities."

"I don't know, Alison. It kind of happened. I told myself the first time I would only say hi. I thought he deserved it, especially after you let me know he'd been pining for me all those years, but after I met him again, I couldn't stop thinking about him. I told myself it was stupid."

She frowned. "Why would it be stupid?"

"Because neither of us were the same person. I asked Mom, and she gave me some big speech about the universe not always throwing love at us in a way we'd expect, and how she never would have thought in her wildest dreams that she'd end up with an elf who could barely navigate a CVS when they first met." Izzie snickered. "It is kind of weird to think of my dad as the guy who once stumbled around Earth trying to stay undercover."

"I can understand that."

Alison had always known Izzie's father as the Fixer. He'd already been well-adapted to Earth by the time she'd met him, and her mother hadn't been the confused cop coming to terms with the existence of magic. In a real sense, the Earth they had met on no longer existed. Everyone knew about magic and Oriceran now.

"Anyway," her friend continued, "one date became two and then more, and…I guess the old fire is still there."

"I know Luke loves you," she assured her. "He made that much obvious when I visited him in DC, and it was clear even from his office."

"I'm not saying I don't love him, and I honestly feel that maybe I still do, but I also have to face the possibility that I'm deluding myself."

"What do you mean?" Alison asked.

"I spent so many years on the run that the idea of a normal life with normal things like a boyfriend became a distant dream, let alone settling down." Izzie sighed. "I think in the last few years, I began to believe I would never actually be able to have anything like that. Now that the dark wizards aren't breathing down my neck and my family's safe, what if it's only me seeking out what seems like it's easy and there for me? What if I'm holding on to the old feelings because they are easier to reach than meeting someone new with all my baggage?"

"I don't need my soul sight anymore to know that's crap," she replied as she stood. It had turned into a pacing conversation. "You're many things, Izzie, but you're not the kind of woman who deludes herself. If you feel something there, then it's there. Don't pull an Alison Brownstone and try to push it away by overthinking. Before, your excuse was that being around Luke made it too dangerous for him. It's not dangerous for him anymore, and if he loves you and you even think you love him, you at least need to make a serious effort. You both deserve it, and you owe it to both yourself and Luke to try." She chuckled. "Although it sounds like you are already trying."

"You're right." Izzie fell silent for a few seconds. "And it's not like he's deluded. I know how hard I am now compared to what I was like in school and I know he sees it, but he doesn't seem to care. I also understand that he's not the same boy from school. Even if we aren't the same girl and boy, it's not crazy that the new man and woman can be together."

"Exactly," she responded cheerfully.

Her friend chuckled. "You get engaged and suddenly you're Little Miss Cupid."

"Hey, it's not like that. Even before I got engaged, I hoped you two would get together."

"Even though—damn. Forget it. I'm sorry I even brought it up."

Alison frowned at her phone. "Even though what? After everything we've been through, Izzie, now's not the time to shut me out."

"Even though you didn't get back together with Tanner?" Uncertainly clouded her voice.

"Yes," she responded without even a hint of hesitation. "That situation is different. Tanner was stalled in a way that Luke wasn't. He was still the same boy when he woke from the coma, and I wasn't the same girl. It would never have worked, and he understood that. Last time I heard, he was seeing someone and I'm glad for him."

"You're absolutely sure?"

"That's one thing I am sure about." She managed a smile, stopped pacing, and dropped onto the couch. "Just because I've been slow about letting go of the past doesn't mean I haven't achieved some of it. I might be the Princess of Overthinking, but I still win in the end."

"Good, good." Izzie took a deep breath. "And everything else is okay? You, your people, and your dad gave me my life back and took a major threat away from my parents, too. And don't think for a second that I don't constantly remember that Myna died because of it."

Alison sighed. "Yes, she did. I try to tell myself she was close to death anyway and she died defending a city, but it only dulls the pain. Still, that's not your fault, Izzie. It's the Seventh Order's fault, and we made them pay."

"I understand that. The point is I owe you and everyone you brought along, Alison. I owe you a debt that I'm not sure I can ever fully repay, and I'm a woman who likes to settle her debts. Taking on a powerful dark wizard faction isn't something you can brush away with 'That's what friends are for.'"

"But that is exactly what friends are for. Especially friends you made at a magic school and who already went through trouble together with you from dark wizards. You don't owe me anything, Izzie. I helped you because I wanted to. It's as simple as that."

Izzie muttered something under her breath. "Do you promise me there's no trouble right now?"

No, you don't, Izzie. I won't let you.

"I run a security company," Alison replied and kept her

tone light. "I always have trouble. It's part of the job description."

"You know what I mean. Something more serious." The woman's voice tightened. "Like crazy billionaires or dark wizards."

"I'm fine. You don't need to worry about me. I didn't have to spend years on the run. You deserve a vacation for the next twenty years. Concentrate on hanging out with your family or surfing with Yumfuck."

Izzie barked out a laugh. "Surfing with Yumfuck? I'll have to ask him about that."

She wasn't sure if the troll enjoyed surfing, but he had taken to Earth in many ways. It wasn't impossible.

"I'm only saying you don't need to worry about me," she explained. "I literally have an entire building full of highly trained people who watch my back, including my boyfriend, a life wizard with years of bodyguard experience. I have an army on call to fight my enemies."

"I feel like you're holding something back, but I can't say you're wrong, either. And we both know that with one phone call, you could have the ultimate weapon and barbecue enthusiast up there."

Alison's mouth quirked into a smile. "That's true, too. Enjoy your time off. Go out on more dates with Luke. Go on a romantic weekend with him."

"Enjoy my time off?" Izzie mused. "It's harder than you think."

"Why is that?"

"Because I don't know how to fill my days," she admitted. "I'm used to bounty hunting or following dark wizard leads. I've even done a few quick bounties here and there simply because I don't know what else to do."

"And do you enjoy it?" She couldn't help the doubt that crept into her voice.

"I think I developed a liking for dealing with scumbags over the years. There are worse addictions. At least satisfying my cravings ends with the world a slightly better place."

Light footsteps sounded from the stairs and Alison looked over her shoulder. A yawning Sonya arrived at the bottom of the stairs and gave her a blank, heavy-lidded stare before she headed toward the kitchen. It must have been snack time.

"If I understand correctly," Alison replied, "you go out on dates with Luke, the only boy—uh, man—you've ever loved, and you eliminate a few scumbags in the meantime."

"That's about right."

"Are you happy?"

Izzie hesitated. "I think so. I really do. And you?"

"I'm getting married and my company's doing well. What reason do I have to not be happy?"

Her friend snorted. "For all I know, you could have some mysterious enemy hunting you."

Technically, the Tapestry is hunting Omni, not me.

"Even if they were, they'd end up exactly the same as the Seventh Order, the Harriken, and everyone else who has screwed with a Brownstone or a Berens."

Izzie uttered a dark chuckle. "I'm sure they would. And it's a good thing. It sounds like life is going well for both of us."

Alison took a deep breath and released it slowly.

Focusing on what she could control was her only real option. "Yes, it is. I'm glad for you, Izzie."

"And I'm glad for you, Alison. It sounds like both of us are finally able to live the lives we wanted after school."

She let that sink in. It was true. Her job was dangerous and she would never deny that, but she used her power to make the world safer.

"I'll let you know what'll happen with the wedding," she added cheerfully.

CHAPTER FOUR

I t took a certain kind of man to work with dead bodies on a daily basis. Gary believed he fit the mold and had for a couple of decades. In that time, he had always attempted to maintain a professional distance as a mortician and focused on performing his job with skill and decorum. Even the return of magic, despite all its wonders of healing, couldn't stop death. Someday, he hoped to prepare a gnome's body.

The professional pride that fueled him was the only thing that prevented him from immediately leaving his office, getting into his car, and going to a bar to get shit-faced drunk after the disturbing story told by his assistant.

"You're not screwing with me, are you?" he asked with a frown. He gripped the edge of his desk tightly and prayed that a practical joke was the explanation. It would be annoying, but it would at least be tolerable.

The other man shook his head. "Why would I screw with you about something like this?"

"Because it becomes unsettling to constantly work on

bodies? I wouldn't blame you if you wanted to play a little joke on me. Simply because I don't like the black humor doesn't mean I expect that no one will ever use it." He pinched the bridge of his nose. "But the joke needs to end. I'm not in the mood."

His assistant shook his head. "This is no joke. The bodies are all gone." His mouth twitched. "Let me rephrase that. Not all of them—not the ones we were prepping for burial after services—but all the bodies that were supposed to be cremated are gone."

Gary stared at his colleague and searched his face for any hint of a lie, but all he saw was concern, which in turn fueled his own. "Where did they go?"

The man shrugged. "Your guess is as good as mine. They have simply vanished."

"Eight bodies don't get up and walk away," he snapped. "They're dead, and dead people don't leave a funeral home unless they're carried out."

"Are you so sure?" He raised an eyebrow.

"Yes, I'm sure they were dead, and the people who brought them here were also sure. Give me a freaking break."

"You don't understand me." His assistant shook his head. "You can't be sure they didn't walk away. Think about it. No one likes to talk about it, and they're rare, but necromancers are out there." He shuddered. "Remember that thing in France ten or so years back? Didn't they have to call in the army or something like that? And there have been more than a few incidents since then."

Gary closed his eyes. "I've done this job for twenty-five years. It used to be so much simpler. Now, we have to also work with non-human bodies and worry about dead people getting up." He opened his eyes slowly. "This is ridiculous. The dead should stay dead. I don't give a shit about some wizard's hocus pocus."

"What do we do?" his colleague asked. "Call the cops? The FBI? The PDA? The health department?"

He shook his head. "If we admit those bodies are gone, it means we'll have to give refunds, and it's not like the families will double-check the ash."

The man nodded, resignation on his face. "I think I can sprinkle some bone fragments from some of the other cremations around."

"Good." Gary stood and headed to the door of his office.

"Uh, where are you going?"

"I give up. I need a drink."

The mortician finished his fifth beer with a huge gulp. He slammed the mug down and the warmth stirred by the drink continued to suffuse his body while the fog spread in his mind. "Thanks for coming, Cliff. I needed someone to talk to who would understand, mortician to mortician."

A dour, stout middle-aged man sat across from him in a corner booth, a slight frown on his face. Unlike his conversation partner, he was still nursing his first beer.

"I half-suspected missing bodies were what you wanted to talk to me about."

"Really?"

"Yes." Cliff's gaze darted warily around the room. "It happened to me, too."

He stared at his companion as the words pushed through the thick miasma in his mind. "W-what?"

The man leaned forward. "I'm saying it happened to me, too. Exactly the same thing. I'm missing bodies. I checked my surveillance cameras, and they malfunctioned for a few minutes. In that few-minute window, someone made off with my bodies."

"When was this?"

"About two weeks ago."

Gary stared longingly into his empty mug. "I didn't hear anything about it on the news," he ventured. "The cops must have kept it awfully quiet for you. That's nice."

"I didn't tell them," he whispered. He looked around for a moment before he leaned forward. "Things have been rough this year, especially with my divorce. I can't give all that money back."

"I know what you mean. There's too much competition and all those stupid natural burials." He sighed. "But what if it isn't only you and me? That means they'll probably do the same at other places. Someone will talk." He shook a finger. "Like Hirano. If they steal his, he'll go to the cops. He's always going off all snooty about his family running some shrine in Japan. I never liked him. He thinks he's better than us."

Cliff shrugged. "Maybe it's only a coincidence. It could be nothing."

He took a deep breath. "You don't think it's necromancers, do you? My assistant suggested it could be them."

"No. That's silly. Sure, they're out there, but no necromancer will go around robbing a number of different funeral homes." The man gestured around the room. "Think about it. Every corpse they steal raises the chance of them getting caught and then, the cops or the bounty hunters move in. Or even the Dark Princess."

"Alison Brownstone?" Gary's forehead wrinkled in confusion. "What does she care about bodies?"

"Her dad has eliminated several necromancers. Mexico, Chile, Detroit, to name only a few. I read this article about him. Like father, like daughter, you know."

"Then, if that's the case, we don't have to worry. She'll take care of the problem for us." He bit his lip. "But on the other hand, what if we're wrong? What if there's a group of zombies in the Underground now?"

"Then Brownstone, the AET, or the PDA will handle it." Cliff nodded with an exaggerated display of wisdom. To Gary, the motion made the whole room seem to sway with him. "If there actually is a necromancer and we make a noise about it, he might come and kill us and make us zombies, too. Do you want that?"

"Of course not." He gritted his teeth and grimaced. "But can we ignore this?"

"Why can't we?" Cliff shrugged. "Every day in this city, crimes happen to the living. Do you think that every person who sees them goes straight to the cops, or do you think they mind their own business?" He pointed to himself, then Gary. "This is where we mind our own business. We didn't do anything wrong."

"But the bodies...the cremations."

"We offer peace of mind, Gary, right? That's the role we play in this whole ecosystem of death."

Gary frowned at the lack of a nearby waitress. He wasn't nearly drunk enough.

"A priest or pastor might offer words of comfort," his companion continued, "but we do the dirty work to make sure that in the end, the family's comfortable with the passing of a loved one. Do you think any of the families would be comfortable if we told them their loved ones' bodies had gone missing? Do you want to rob them of that?"

"But...they could be zombies," he countered.

"Could isn't the same thing as are." The man nodded, apparently satisfied with his brilliant logic. "We could be wrong and this is merely some stupid prank."

"The bodies are gone," Gary all but shouted. He winced, but the cacophony of the crowded bar and the lack of anyone near the table saved them both.

"Or it could simply be good, old-fashioned body-snatchers," his friend suggested. "Maybe someone's hoping to sell the organs. Not everyone has access to affordable magical healing or a decent transplant. We can't assume it's necromancers. It's irresponsible to do that, and it's also irresponsible to shirk our duty to the families. We need to continue to provide peace of mind. The rest will sort itself out, whether it's simply a prank or because of Hirano or some other fool who doesn't understand the bigger picture."

Gary waved at a waitress across the room. She offered him a smile but held up a tray of empty drinks before she headed toward a back room. He muttered a few obscenities.

"That makes sense," he admitted with a jerk of his head.

"If it is a necromancer, they have magic spells that will confuse tracking anyway. It's not like even if we told the cops, they would be able to find them." His gaze followed the progress of the waitress across the room and into the back.

"Yes. The only logical choice is to sit tight and continue as normal."

"You're right. It is what it is." Gary smiled as the waitress emerged once again and moved toward their table.

"Exactly," Cliff replied. "I'm sure this will all turn out to be nothing important at all. Even in a city as crazy as this one, a few missing bodies doesn't mean anything special's going on."

CHAPTER FIVE

Alison stifled a yawn as she looked around the conference room table at her core magical team. Insomnia had struck her hard as of late, seeded by her spending far too long talking to Izzie a few days earlier. If the problem continued, she would have to consider energy potions or a spell but using magic to replace a true good night's rest carried risks of its own. Magic might bend reality here and there, but reality tended to sneak in when she least expected it.

Maybe I need more of a break than I realized—an actual long vacation. It's not like Seattle will disappear if I take a month off. At least I hope it won't.

Ava cleared her throat from beside her. "Per your request, all the secondary background checks are in order, Miss Brownstone."

"Good. I wanted to be extra careful considering what's involved with this."

Hana looked up from her nails. "So what's the job? Why do we need to be extra careful?"

Drysi and Mason leaned forward with interest, but Tahir wore the same detached expression of vague disinterest he typically presented during a briefing, a false mask to pretend he didn't care about something he would probably spend days following up on later.

We're all less closed off, but that doesn't mean all the habits we developed before meeting each other aren't still there.

"It's a quick job," Alison began. "It'll take a couple of days at most, and the second day shouldn't be anything more than traveling back to Seattle."

She nodded at Ava. The administrative assistant tapped her tablet and a life-sized hologram of a painting appeared above the table. The image depicted a complex series of interconnected stairs, all of which originated from a vast ocean and ended at the base of seven towers under two suns. The structures were composed of different materials —glass, stone, wood, copper, silver, gold, and crystal. A variety of different beings populated the tops of the towers, including humans and angels in some but also elves, gnomes, and a few other Oriceran races in others. Closer inspection revealed Arpaks mixed amongst the angels. Intricate brushwork and attention to detail and perspective gave the painting an almost photo-realistic quality.

"This is *Axis Omnium Mundos*," Alison explained. "It's a long-lost magical painting by Leonardo da Vinci. It's been rumored to exist for twenty years, but most people thought it was a myth, something made up after the gates opened."

"Magical?" Drysi pointed at the image. "Someone enchanted a da Vinci?"

"Yes. He did."

Drysi raised an eyebrow. "So it's true? The bloody bastard was a wizard?"

She nodded. "It's been suspected because of a few enchantments here and there on other paintings, but this finding is considered the confirmation of what was long suspected, as you said, that da Vinci was a wizard. Even when they found that journal last year, many people weren't sure."

"I always thought it was made up," Mason admitted with a shrug. "The minute the gates started opening, people tried to claim every famous person in history was a magical."

"Someone went through a lot of trouble to try to hide the fact he was a wizard, even from magicals, but that's not important considering he's been dead for a long time." She inclined her head at the painting. "But this painting is important, and it's the job."

"I don't understand," Hana replied. "How is a painting a security job?"

Alison gestured toward the image again. "They have a high-value courier taking the painting from where it's being stored in Seattle, which is currently a hidden vault. It was originally found during an inventory of the estate of a wealthy art collector who recently passed away. The woman who inherited it suspected it was extraordinary, so she brought specialists in."

"How do we know it's not a fake?" Mason asked. "A half-decent wizard could create a painting and slap a few enchantments on it."

She shrugged. "I don't know all the details, but it's already been authenticated through non-magical and magical means. Our job is to support the courier. He'll actually be handling the artwork, and he's taking it from the vault to a magical research facility in San Francisco. It's run by a group of art magic researchers, the Magical Art Research Society. They call themselves MARS for short. They are technically our clients and the ones responsible for authenticating the painting."

"MARS?" The fox chuckled. "Cute. I wonder if they did that on purpose."

Tahir tore his gaze away from the painting. "If they're hiring us in addition to a courier, it means this painting is especially valuable. Given how much some previous lost da Vincis sold for, I can imagine it would garner a rather hefty price."

"Yep." Alison took a deep breath. "According to MARS, it could easily bring in two billion at auction. Maybe considerably more."

Hana bolted from her seat. "Two billion dollars?" she shouted. "Billions with a b?"

Drysi whistled.

Alison nodded. "Yeah. The woman who inherited it is actually giving it to MARS as a tax write-off. She doesn't want to deal with the hassle of protecting something that valuable. From what they've said, they're worried about that issue themselves, but they have additional means once it reaches San Francisco. After all, they're all magicals."

"I can see how something that valuable might freak someone out," Mason replied. "But why even bother with a courier? Why not simply portal it directly? It's still at risk this way."

"They've already tried that," she explained. "Every

portal they summon collapses once the painting gets within a few feet. They're not sure if it's a deliberate defensive enchantment or a side-effect of other spells."

"And it's not simply anti-magic in general?"

She shook her head. "No. Most other magic works on and around it, but they can't create a stable portal and they're too afraid to try to push more magic into one as it might collapse while the painting's halfway through. They're also afraid to fly it because they have no idea if its sensitive to altitude or might disable the plane somehow, but they do know that it can be transported by car without anything weird happening." Her jaw tightened. "Assuming no one tries to take it."

Drysi folded her arms over her chest. "The courier takes the painting, and we eliminate any thieves who show up? That seems simple enough."

"That's the general idea. They've used the courier before, but they've never had anything this valuable so they're taking extra precautions. No one wants to lose their chance to examine something like this. They claim the painting might be the key to understanding some of the other enchantments that have been discovered on da Vinci paintings, especially when combined with information from the journal."

"What about threats?" Tahir inquired, his eyes alight with enthusiasm, any hint of feigned disinterest long gone. "Something worth billions has to have attracted considerable attention from the greedy and the violent."

"Everyone involved has tried to keep it quiet," Alison explained. "The painting also has inherent anti-tracking magic. Not only that, the local MARS contacts will place it in an enchanted sleeve with additional protections. Without a direct sample of the painting, it'll be all but impossible for anyone to track it magically. It's not impossible that something leaked, though, but at least it'll be harder for them to follow up on it."

"They've done a good job of keeping it out of the news," Hana observed. "Otherwise, I think we would have heard something about a painting worth a couple of billion or more. Isn't hiring us overkill in that case, or did it leak and they're still trying to keep it quiet?"

Tahir frowned as he considered this. "If it did leak, even the criminals who might possibly be involved haven't said anything. I haven't seen anything on the dark web to suggest anyone knows about this painting. I don't even remember the last time I read about it. It was probably last year."

"It's like you said, Hana," Alison clarified. "This painting is worth an enormous amount of money. It's also a unique magical artwork by a great historical figure who most people, even magicals, didn't even suspect was a wizard until recently. No matter how careful everyone tries to be, word might leak out even if it hasn't already, and once it does, the risk goes up substantially."

Mason uttered a quiet grunt. "It's the same reason I always hated celebrity bodyguard jobs. Inevitably, someone involved can't help themselves. They always have to tell a friend to make themselves feel special." He sighed. "So what's the plan? I assume we won't do this as a massive parade. A show of force is great, but all it takes is a thief with good mobility and timing, and they escape with what you virtually described as an untraceable painting."

"First of all, this will be a mixed mission," she explained. "I want a few more bodies guarding the painting, so I'll bring on a few of Jerry's team. At the same time, if we barrel down the highway in a massive convoy, it'll be a huge red flag to anyone watching. So, we'll use a small team of non-magical personnel to supplement our core group. That will be led by Amelia. She might be fairly new here, but she has a strong background and Jerry personally recommended her for both initial hiring and this job. I assume no one has a problem with that?"

She looked around the table, but everyone shook their heads. "We'll take the SUVs, and Amelia's team will be equipped with full anti-magic gear. We have to assume that anyone who tries to take a painting this valuable is willing to kill a few people along the way, and I refuse to risk any of my people through lack of preparation." She nodded to Ava, and a moment later, a road map of the west coast appeared. "It's fairly simple. We'll set out early morning and drive straight down. We'll carry food. Otherwise, it's merely the occasional trip to the bathroom and battery charging. Both Sonya and Tahir will provide active support the entire time. I know it's a long time, but it's only the one day."

Hana tilted her head as she studied the map. "And how long exactly is it from Seattle to San Francisco?"

"With a few quick breaks and charging times, we should be able to do it in about thirteen and a half hours," she replied. "It's essentially a direct trip down I-5. Unless we have intelligence to indicate otherwise, we'll avoid leaving the most direct route."

"Guarding a painting, huh?" Mason grinned. "I've

guarded a variety of people and artifacts, but I don't think I've ever protected something this valuable before."

"Let's hope this ends up an easy job," Alison responded with a smile. "It's a nice payday for one day's work." Her smile faded. "I do think you should stay here, though, Hana."

The fox frowned. "Why?"

"If this job does somehow leak, it could mean the Tapestry might get wind of it," she explained. "And they might think it's an opportunity to snatch Omni. Most of the staff will still be here, but I'd like at least one magical. Between you, Ava, and the rest of the team, you would be able to hold them off long enough for AET to arrive. You might be able to coax Omni into his battle form if necessary, too. Plus, we can't really bring him along. That presents two tempting targets."

Hana shrugged. "That's fine by me. Sitting in a car for half the day sounds boring anyway."

CHAPTER SIX

Mason had the wheel with Alison in the passenger seat as they cruised down the highway in one of her company's unmarked armored SUVs. Her muscles remained tight, especially those in her neck. She couldn't seem to allow herself to relax and they were only a few hours into the trip.

If I keep this up, I'll be ridiculously sore tonight, even if no one comes to kill us and make off with the painting. Is it really only the job? No, there's something else there.

Drysi traveled with Amelia and her team in a second SUV. Alison thought it was important for them to have additional magical backup, and she hadn't worked as closely with some of the non-magical employees as the rest of the main team had.

Wait. I know what has me so tense.

"The Tapestry bugs me," she declared and broke a long stretch of silence between her and Mason. "Really, really bugs me."

He shot her a grin. "It's not like anyone likes them. I bet

they don't even like each other much. I don't think anyone will complain that you're not their biggest fans."

She sighed. "No, it's like—forgive the pun—but it's like they're this loose strand I want to cut because every time I tug on it, I pull out more thread. We might have stopped Ultimate, but they had to be behind it, and yet they managed to hide during that whole thing. It's frustrating. They've been too damned quiet, and I refuse to believe, after everything they've done, that they're willing to give up on Omni so easily, even if we ended their little Ultimate experiment."

Mason performed a quick camera and mirror check. "Sure, that's all true, but look at the Seventh Order. They were willing to wait a long time between their stunts, either because they were patient or because they needed more time to build up their forces. For all we know, the Tapestry might try again next week, or they might wait a year before their next move. They aren't the first loose end we've had to deal with at the company, and not your first, for sure."

"Yeah, with my luck, they'll wait until our honeymoon," Alison grumbled. "I honestly thought we would find them at the end of all that crap last month."

He laughed. "Just so you know, if we're on our honeymoon, I won't leave, no matter what. I don't care if the Tapestry floods the US with Strands. Hell, that Nine Systems Alliance could invade the Earth, and I'd simply say, 'Hey, we'll join the resistance after we get back from our honeymoon.'"

"Don't worry. In that case, my dad will handle them. He'll protect our honeymoon."

"Good to know." He grinned. "I need my Alison time."

She snickered. "Priorities, huh? The freedom of the Earth comes second to spending time with me?"

"Yes." He winked. "There's no greater priority than you, and you don't seem like you're going to enslave the Earth anytime soon, so it's not like I have to make any hard calls. My point is, don't worry about the Tapestry for now. They'll show their face eventually, and when they do, we'll tear it off."

She turned away, her cheeks burning. "I only...want some leads, is all. I feel like all we need is one last push and we could finish them off. If they haven't attacked us again, it means they're weak. I'm not Miar or Rasila and I'm not obsessed with some great personal challenge. I simply want to remove criminals when I have a chance to do so, and I have a feeling that between the earlier ass-kicking we gave them and by messing up the Ultimate being dealt in Seattle, we have them primed for our knock-out blow."

Mason nodded. "That's all true, but right now, they aren't the problem and we have no real leads. The painting is the job, and I doubt the Tapestry will show up to steal it. Whatever their motivation is, it doesn't really seem to be about money."

Alison shook her head. "Speaking of money, this whole thing is still hard to wrap my head around. It's one thing to auction off or sell a valuable painting legally, but the logistics involved in trying to move something like that underground blows my mind. It's not like you can put up an ad on the internet, even the dark web, without placing a huge target on your back for everyone from the government to criminal groups. Even Lily and Mom, when they have to move artifacts, usually sell them to someone who hired them to begin with. There is no way either of them could move a billion-dollar artifact without half the world finding out."

He grunted and suspicion colored his face. "You're presupposing that any thieves will steal the artifact and look for a buyer later."

"You don't think that's how it would go down?"

"Someone could hire thieves specifically to steal the painting. Any number of criminals would be interested in an upfront payment that doesn't involve all the legwork of trying to actually move the painting itself."

She frowned. "True enough."

"Stealing expensive artwork has gone on for a long time, magical or not," he continued. "Sometimes, some rich asshole merely wants to have something special sitting in his basement to show off to his friends, and he doesn't care how he got it." He glanced at the rearview camera and the courier's SUV that carried the painting. "I hope I can at least sneak a peek. It's not often I get so close to something like that."

"I noticed that you haven't been painting as much lately," Alison commented.

"Despite having such a great muse?" He smiled. "Are you insulted?"

"I only hope everything's okay," she explained. "I don't want you to give up something you love to do."

Mason shook his head. "It's fine. We've been busy with work, moving in together, and other stuff, whether Ultimate or even me planning my proposal, but you're right. I do want to get back into painting more. I simply need to carve out the time and being in the presence of a magical da Vinci serves as extra inspiration. It's not you or the job, A. It's merely how things have worked out these last few months."

"We have extra rooms at the house," she pointed out. "You can convert one of those to a full studio, rather than put an easel up wherever."

He smiled. "I might actually do that. Having the space might be a good inspiration in and of itself."

"We have trouble," Sonya announced through their ear receivers.

Alison tapped her ear to start transmitting. "Trouble? What trouble?"

"Several cars raced up a nearby onramp and are closing on you, all black Mazdas with tinted windows," the girl explained. "The plates are all stolen."

"Stolen? How do you know?" she asked.

"Because they are registered to different cars than the ones I see—different makes and models."

She snorted. "I suppose it was too much to hope for a quiet job when billions of dollars are on the line. Tahir, do you see anything else?"

"I can confirm the vehicles," he replied. "There are no other drones or aircraft nearby."

Mason's hands tightened around the wheel. "Money always complicates things."

CHAPTER SEVEN

"Magicals confirmed," Tahir commented. "There are spells around all four cars. I can't get a thermal profile with the drones, and they've actively blocked my scrying. That means they have at least one wizard with them."

"Not a huge surprise," Alison muttered. "And I assume it's far more than one wizard. To send a purely non-magical team after something like this painting is simply asking to have your ass kicked. Even if they don't know we're involved, they would have to assume that magical security would be provided for a magical painting."

"I do feel compelled to note there's a small possibility they're someone who really likes their privacy," the info-mancer observed. A faint hint of mirth lingered in his tone.

I'm glad someone finds this funny, but it's not like I can afford to pay them back if I damage their two-billion-dollar painting.

"I would love for that to be true, but I doubt it." She

sighed. "Okay, Mason will pull back. Amelia, you and the courier should pull forward."

During their previous conversations, the courier agreed to follow her orders, but agreeing to do something and actually doing it were two separate things.

Don't do something stupid, and we'll be fine.

"Copy that, Alison," Amelia replied.

"Fine with me," the courier added.

Okay. I can work with this.

Mason nodded without taking his gaze off the road. He switched lanes and eased up on the accelerator to allow the SUV to drift naturally behind the other two vehicles in the small convoy. A stream of cars passed them in the far lane.

Alison looked out the front and back windows. "There are still too many cars on the road. If we get into a fight here, we could cause a serious accident and innocent people will be hurt." She frowned. "Tahir, what does it look like at the next exit?"

"I don't see any suspicious vehicles there," he reported.

"Are there any buildings nearby?"

"Not for a few miles. There's a small store and gas station several miles up the road."

She exhaled a sigh of relief. "Okay then, that seals it. We'll keep the same formation and take the next exit. Whoever is following us has some restraints too, and we can use that against them."

"And what are those?" Drysi asked.

"This isn't a hit," she explained. "It's a theft. They're here for the painting. If they're too rough, they risk damaging it, and it's not like they can dig up da Vinci and force him to paint a new one."

The Welsh witch snickered over the connection.

"It means that once we're clear of the main highway and potential collateral damage, we can actually play this a little rougher than they can." She grinned. "Sometimes, it's nice to be the one who doesn't have to hold back. We'll have to decide where to stop before we reach the gas station, but I think we have the advantage."

"The cars are closing on you fast," Sonya reported. "You should be able to see them now."

Alison alternated her attention between the rearview mirror and camera. The four Mazdas hurtled up the highway in a column and wove in and out of the traffic.

It's a good thing we're getting off the road. They'll cause a wreck simply with that erratic driving.

The convoy reached the exit, which took them along the edge of a tall forest. A dirt road veered into the trees, a possible path toward reducing collateral damage, at least to humans.

"Okay, I think what we should do—" she began.

The SUV suddenly died. The two other vehicles moved away, but their lights both faded a few seconds later.

"What the hell?" Alison shouted. "Tahir, what happened?"

There was no response.

She tapped at her ear. "Tahir?" She looked at Mason.

He shook his head. "I don't hear anything." He pressed the brakes lightly and brought the SUV to a stop behind the other two vehicles.

Even though Tahir's receivers were aided by magic and possessed range and capability far beyond normal communications gear, they were still fundamentally electronic devices and not magical artifacts, meaning they shared certain vulnerabilities with the SUV—weaknesses she hadn't prepared for in this job.

I assumed they would strike with a big and obvious spell of some kind.

Alison scrubbed a hand down her face. "Of course. What do you do when you need to stop someone but can't risk shooting at them? You EMP them." She summoned a shield and threw the door open. "I was smart enough to EMP-proof my phone, but not our vehicles. We can fix them with a few minutes and magic, but we might as well make our stand now. At least this way, there's less risk to the forest."

"That's one way to think of it." Mason cast his shield and enhancement spells before he exited the vehicle. She conjured a shadow blade and crouched behind the back of the disabled SUV. Taking the hint, Drysi exited the front of her vehicle, a gun in hand, but her other hand hovered inside her jacket over one of her sheathed knives. Amelia stepped out and her red ponytail swayed with the movement. Four of the other security personnel left the SUV as well. All wore anti-magic deflectors around their necks and held pistols already drawn. Stun rods hung from their belts. They'd all been cleared to load anti-magic bullets into their weapons. It would be an expensive battle if it wasn't over quickly.

The courier didn't exit his vehicle.

The four sedans following them turned, and the tires squealed noisily as they halted. The doors flew open on both sides and a dozen men poured out, all holding wands and shouting.

Huh. I expected a few wizards but not twelve. These guys have gone all out. Then again, this is for billions of dollars.

Four of the men lifted their wands to conjure a shimmering wall in front of their vehicles. Not only were there a large number of magicals, but they were used to working together.

"You don't have to get hurt here," one of them called to the security team. "Hand over the painting, and we'll be on our way. Refuse, and we'll kill every last one of you to take it. We outnumber you."

Alison scoffed. "There's no way we'll give that painting up, and I'm sure we can kick your asses."

"So be it," he shouted.

A barrage of blue-black bolts followed.

Life-draining magic.

Alison narrowed her eyes. That kind of spell was more difficult to achieve than a rapid elemental attack like a fireball or ice lance. It was further proof they weren't dealing with cheap magical thugs. The Brownstone personnel stayed low and avoided the attacks, which instead, struck their vehicles and dissipated without causing any damage.

She replied by pelting the shield with a few bolts of her light magic to weaken it. Mason, Drysi, Amelia, and the others opened fire with their pistols and took a few careful shots. The massive shimmering shield slowed the anti-magic ammunition but didn't stop it. Bullets struck windows and spider-webbed cracks spread from the point of impact. One wizard groaned and collapsed after taking a round in the shoulder. He might not be severely injured by the slower projectile, but no one wanted a piece of metal in their shoulder.

They underestimated us because they didn't see many wands.

A couple of the attackers pointed their wands and yelled. Slabs of asphalt ripped from the road in a zigzag pattern stretching toward the Brownstone vehicles. The enemy was making their own cover.

Alison continued to hammer away at the shield with a stream of light bolts until the spell finally dissipated, unable to absorb any more damage. She took a few deep breaths and her eyes narrowed on the thieves.

Some of the men darted forward with quick point-to-point movement from the cars to the asphalt barriers. They covered their advance with a variety of life bolts and fireballs. Drysi grunted as a blue-black bolt struck her shield. Another assailant was struck by a fireball. His anti-magic deflector darkened slightly, but his only sign of pain was a grunt.

Time to encircle these guys and finish them off.

Alison charged forward and her shield absorbed a few life bolts and fireballs before she ducked behind one of the thieves' new asphalt shields. She powered magic into her legs and released it to fling herself forward and up. Half the enemy still remained near their vehicles. They jerked their wands up to fire at the leaping woman but most of their shots missed. The few fireballs that landed stung but didn't accomplish much else.

She landed behind a thief and slashed at his shield. He spun to face her, his eyes wide in panic, but his defenses fell after a few blows, and she stabbed him through the chest. Two more nearby went down as Mason delivered rounds into them. One took a bullet to the head, the other to the chest.

Ava will yell at me later for the cost of this job.

With a grim smile, she summoned another blade in her other hand, put more magic into her shields, and bellowed a challenge. She rushed toward the remaining thieves near the cars. Their barriers didn't hold up for long when she thrust and sliced in earnest. Mason's suppressive fire distracted the wizards, who only managed a few glancing strikes against her shields before she felled them with a flurry of rapid attacks.

Drysi threw an enchanted dagger into the makeshift barrier behind which the approaching wizards sheltered. An explosion destroyed one section of their cover and several of the men staggered. Amelia and the other team members took their opportunity to fire and annihilated the men in a hail of anti-magic bullets. The surprised looks on some of their faces suggested they still hadn't registered exactly what they were dealing with.

Alison had finished with the men at the cars and rounded on the few surviving thieves who remained crouched behind asphalt barriers. She released her shadow blades and flung her arm out to launch a shadow crescent. The magical weapon pounded into the back of a wizard's shield. He groaned and turned. The attack hadn't penetrated completely, but one of Amelia's bullets found the back of his now exposed head.

The last survivor raised his hands and tossed his wand aside as he glared at her. "I'll remember this."

"Really? That's the line you're going with?" She pointed toward Amelia and her team. "We didn't even take a serious injury and half your team is dead. Maybe you shouldn't threaten someone who obviously outclasses you."

She shook her head and strengthened her shield. "Cuff him. I'm sure the police will want to talk to them."

He scoffed. "They'll get nothing out of me."

"I don't care. You'll rot in jail for attacking us anyway. Maybe, just maybe, if you want to get out of prison before King Oriceran grows old, you'll find some reason to be helpful to the authorities. If not, I don't care." She smirked. "I'll live a long Drow life satisfied with the knowledge that you're in prison."

The thief's mouth twitched, but he lowered his head, defeat in his eyes.

Amelia and her team rushed forward, their guns at the ready. They surrounded the wizard before she shoved him to his knees and removed his handguns. She kicked his wand away.

Alison surveyed the men who sprawled on the blood-stained road. Some had long since stopped breathing. Others groaned quietly, survivors of the battle but in need of medical care.

"Mason, stabilize anyone still breathing," she ordered. "The rest of you, cuff them while he works on them." She gestured to the road and the SUVs. "Drysi, can you get them running again?"

The witch nodded. "It'll take a few minutes. It's easier when they don't actually blow things up so it'll be a right tidy fix. You'll never know they were hit."

"And the road?"

Drysi shrugged. "That shouldn't be too difficult."

"I'll help you with that in a minute." Alison retrieved her phone and shook it. "This is still working." She frowned and shook her head. "We were lucky they didn't try something more dangerous. I know they had to protect the painting, but criminals do stupid things all the time."

The courier stepped out of his SUV where he had remained during the entire bottle. The suited man adjusted his sunglasses before he jogged toward her, his lips pressed together.

"We need to move," he insisted. "Now."

She nodded toward a downed thief. "We can't leave them here. We need to wait until the cops come to make sure they don't get away. The ones still alive, at least."

He frowned. "And now we're sitting ducks if they have reinforcements. They know our forces and our capabilities, and if they're watching, they probably even know where the painting is."

Alison looked up and squinted. There were a few black dots high in the sky, but she assumed those were Tahir's drones.

"I understand what you're saying." She waved to Drysi at the vehicles. "Prioritize fixing the SUV with the painting. The rest of you will stay here until the police arrive, and Mason and I will go with our friend here to make the delivery."

"Are you sure that's a good idea, Alison?" Amelia asked and frowned at the courier. "What if there's another ambush?"

"Twelve skilled wizards are already an expensive team to put together," she pointed out. She gestured toward the man who had surrendered. "I doubt they have a whole other team on standby. If they had, they would commit immediately for such a valuable prize. Since they can't track it, their best bet is to come here, which again is more reason why you should watch the prisoners until the police come."

Drysi hurried toward the SUV that held the painting, her wand out as she muttered something under her breath in Welsh.

The courier's frown turned into a slight smile. "Good. We still have a schedule to keep. I understand your position on these thieves, Miss Brownstone, but the sooner we drop this painting off, the less risk to everyone, including innocent bystanders."

"I know." She pointed to the SUV. "You drive. Mason and I will make sure that no other wizards make this an annoying trip." She dialed nine-one-one. "And now to get the cops here."

CHAPTER EIGHT

The MARS staff opened the back of the SUV and Alison exhaled a sigh of relief. The painting lay in a black sleeve ringed with several glowing wards and nestled safely in the same padded box she had seen the Seattle MARS staff place it in. She almost convinced herself that even though there was no obvious damage, the painting would not be inside when they arrived.

Sure, we had to fight off a few wizards, but this wasn't such a bad job.

Despite the trouble they experienced with the wizards, the remainder of the trip passed without incident other than a minor accident blocking traffic a few miles away from the MARS facility. It occupied an otherwise non-descript four-story white building with three sublevels. The heavily warded fence and the various other defensive spells all over the grounds and in and around the building itself might alert a cautious magical that it was far more special than its simple façade suggested.

A cargo elevator had transported the SUV to subbasement two, a cavernous level illuminated by harsh lights from no discernable source. Surrounding the cargo elevator, metal shelving formed a maze filled with sculptures, drawings, paintings, figurines, pottery, and random-looking amalgamations of material that might have been trash or genius art beyond Alison's ability to comprehend.

This actually reminds me of Mom's warehouses. Just because this stuff is art doesn't mean the magic is safe. I wonder how close an eye the government keeps on MARS.

Suits and an excess of bowties exemplified the male MARS staff and long dark skirts clad their female counterparts. The magicals, regardless of gender, kept their wands on belt holsters rather than under their jackets.

Alison stifled a yawn and stretched as two wizards drew the box slowly from the truck as gingerly as if they were handling a bomb. "I'd complain about being achy, but I didn't drive that entire time," she said quietly.

Mason chuckled from beside her. "It's not like you didn't do anything, A. You did help stop a group of wizard thieves who tried to kill us and steal the painting."

"That took a few minutes. The real trouble is in the driving."

The courier grumbled under his breath.

An older witch, who had earlier introduced herself as Carolyn, held her wand above the sleeve as she chanted her spells. Two other wizards stood near her, pensive expressions on their face. One of the wards flashed and vanished in a slow-sizzling column of smoke. She continued with slow deliberation. The incantations took over thirty seconds and the destruction of the wards a good minute apiece.

"Geeze," Alison muttered. "I think this painting's locked down better than anything I've ever done. This is on the level of some of the wards and glyphs that keep the Mountain Strider contained."

"It is worth two billion dollars," Mason murmured in response. "A little extra security is necessary."

"True enough. I've never been this close to something so valuable before. I don't know if I'm supposed to feel different, but I'm mostly only curious."

"I want to see the work of a master. I don't care how much its worth."

The courier stood with his arms folded and tapped his foot, impatience on his face. He'd barely spoken more than a few sentences the entire trip. It was obvious he didn't like having to carpool with a few security contractors. She couldn't help but mess with him by purposefully discussing wedding plans with Mason.

The police had taken a surprisingly long time to arrive —a good hour after her and Mason left—but they now had the survivors in custody and the bodies of the slain. She didn't technically need to stay for the unveiling of the painting, but she wanted him to have his chance to look at it, and his reaction only continued to confirm it.

Carolyn finished the final ward after what seemed like an agonizingly long time. Sweat beaded on her forehead. She whispered another spell and waved her wand over the black sleeve. Two long cuts appeared in it, and it unwound itself to reveal the painting.

Here we go. Two billion dollars.

Mason stared at it, his breathing shallow. Alison thought it didn't look that different than the hologram, but she wasn't an artist so maybe she didn't feel it on the same level as a painter.

Carolyn smiled. "Oh, this is a truly lovely work. We'll be able to learn so much about da Vinci from this. What secrets might it hold? I can only imagine." She pointed her wand for a final spell. The painting glowed a dull green for a few seconds.

The witch's smile vanished, and her lip quivered. "No, no, no."

Alison looked at Mason, but he shrugged, confusion on his face. The courier narrowed his eyes.

The witch cast the spell again. The painting responded with the same dull green light. She took a few ragged breaths before she leaned in to whisper to the two wizards, terror on her face.

"Is there something wrong?" Alison asked and her hands tightened into firsts at her side.

Carolyn swallowed. "Yes, you could say that." She took a deep breath and smoothed her skirt. "It's a fake."

Alison blinked. "Come again?"

She couldn't have said what I think I heard.

The woman pointed her wand at the painting, her eyes narrowed and her jaw tight. "That is not the true *Axis Omnium Mundos.* It does display magic and it's almost a perfect copy visually, but it doesn't display the appropriate resonance. I'm sorry, but it's clearly a fake." Her voice wavered. "As shocking as that is, the truth is undeniable."

The courier's eyes bulged. "What the hell? There's no way it's a fake. Your people verified it."

Alison frowned and nodded. "He's right. The wards weren't put in place by any of my people." She gestured to the courier. "And he's not even a magical. We were both present when your people in Seattle sealed the painting. No one got near it even during the fight, unless you're saying someone managed to go over to a vehicle, while invisible, and dispel all those complex wards in a few minutes while a raging battle took place around them, all the with none of us noticing."

Carolyn sighed. "That's not what I'm suggesting at all. I can assure you of that." She looked at the two wizards. They both nodded.

"Then what are you suggesting?" She tried not to glare but it still manifested. There was no way she would take the blame for this. She wasn't an art expert.

"We agree with your assessment," Carolyn explained, a pained look on her face. "The appropriate and specific wards are all in place, including certain hidden ones I'm doubtful you would have been able to detect even if you somehow could replicate all these specific custom wards in such a short time frame. The painting was obviously already switched before this one was sealed in Seattle." She shook her head. "I would like it if you waited while we checked on a few things. It shouldn't take long. Again, I can assure you that we're not accusing any of you of being responsible."

The courier grunted. "I'm waiting. This could destroy me. I need more details."

Alison shrugged. "I want to know what happened as much as you do."

She wasn't sure if it would destroy her reputation or not. Her job was to protect people, not validate art.

Mason turned and headed toward the entrance to the

shelf maze. "Since we have to wait, we might as well check out the art while we're here."

Despite her disappointment, she couldn't help but chuckle.

A long while later, Alison sat on the floor, one knee up and her back against the wall. Another yawn escaped. She tapped her fingers idly against her knee, waiting for Carolyn to return while Mason continued to explore the art. The courier paced in a tight circle, his face red.

They waited for at least another half-hour before the witch returned, paler than before, and she actually looked ten years older.

"Thank you for waiting," she said apologetically. "I understand how complicated and disconcerting this must be from your perspective, given how distressing it is from ours."

Alison stood. "What exactly is going on?" She had a few theories, but slinging accusations around wouldn't help an already tense situation.

Carolyn tried to smooth her features, but hints of sorrow and anger constantly emerged. "We've verified that one of the MARS researchers assigned to our Seattle branch can't be reached or found, even with magic. This is even though everyone was supposed to ensure they could be reached while we handled the painting."

Alison grimaced. The conclusion all but screamed at them. "You're saying it was an inside job?"

"The evidence would suggest that is the case. It's all but

impossible, even for a woman of your magical talents let alone a non-magical, to have duplicated all those wards without far more time with direct study. And, of course, the sudden disappearance of our research fellow is too coincidental to be ignored."

She frowned. "Maybe something bad has happened to him. He might be a victim, too."

"Perhaps. It's an unfortunate situation when that would almost be the preferred outcome." Carolyn's gaze cut to the sullen courier. "But both of your organizations performed the jobs you were hired to do. You were hired to transport and protect the painting sealed in those wards, and you did as much, up to and including direct physical risk. Accordingly, you will be compensated as per our original agreement, and we'll make it clear to the FBI and any who inquire that the fault is with our organization."

The courier's frown disappeared. He even managed something approaching a smile. "That's fine, then." He waved and headed toward the stairs. "Now I don't feel so bad about using my own vehicle."

Alison forced her attention back to the forlorn-looking witch. "I appreciate you not throwing us under the bus, but that still means somebody got away with a two-billion-dollar magical painting."

"It appears that way." Carolyn's eyes glistened. "This kind of thing is always a risk in my line of work, but this betrayal…and when we were on the cusp of understanding da Vinci's greatest work." She sighed. "I'm an art researcher, not a policewoman, so there is little I can do other than encourage the authorities in their investigation. I also apologize if any aspect of the FBI's investigation troubles you. They have an extreme interest in this case, along with several other government agencies."

"It's not a problem. I'd like a piece of this guy, too. If there is anything I can do or tell them to help them catch the thief, it's fine by me."

"I doubt we'll ever see Ernest again, to be honest." Carolyn's mouth tightened. "If he was brazen enough to do this, it suggests he already has a buyer. Someone with those kinds of resources can afford to hide themselves. Oh, well. I need to break the news to the rest of my organization. This may very well destroy MARS." She turned and shuffled away, her head low. "Thank you again for your efforts. Ironically, we placed all your lives in danger for nothing."

Alison sighed and shook her head.

I don't know how to feel about this. It wasn't my fault, but it still feels like it happened under my watch. Still, I'm not equipped to track an art thief. That is more an FBI job. For now, I need to find Mason so we can get out of here.

CHAPTER NINE

"You're kidding me," Drysi shouted on the other end of the phone. "A bloody inside job? I don't know if I should be impressed or annoyed."

"I've settled on annoyed myself," Alison replied and cradled the phone between her neck and shoulder as she washed her hands in the hotel bathroom. "I think they had nothing to do with the men who attacked us either. They were merely opportunists who were unlucky."

"I almost feel sorry for those bastards we fought against. They risked their lives for nothing." Drysi snorted. "Will you fly back tonight? Or will you find someone to portal you?"

"Nah, we'll fly back tomorrow morning. I've had enough travel for one day. You're all back and safe, and Hana and Ava both said everything was quiet at the building. We might have cut into our budget with our anti-magic bullet use, but we still turned a profit on this job, even though it feels like a hollow victory."

"Not every win can be tidy, Alison," Drysi said firmly.

"And every time you eliminate a criminal, it only makes it that much more likely that the next one will do the smart thing and surrender. Keep that in mind."

"Okay, see you tomorrow, Drysi."

"See you tomorrow."

Alison ended the call and stepped out of the bathroom into the hotel room where Mason sat on the edge of the bed and watched a local news report about integrating magic into the sewage treatment process.

He looked at her. "Is everything okay? You look worried."

"Yeah. We should probably book a flight now." She tossed her phone onto the bed and fell onto the mattress face-first, rolled onto her side, and sighed. "I'm beginning to see the appeal of your eloping and long honeymoon plan, especially if we ignore everything else that's happening during our honeymoon."

Mason grinned. "Exactly." He tapped the side of his head. "I do have a few good ideas now and again, but how about a little practice?"

"What do you mean?" She sat up.

"We don't have a job lined up tomorrow, right?"

"Ava didn't mention anything, and I wouldn't want either our team or Amelia's team to do back-to-back jobs after having to deal with an actual fight," she explained. "We might not have taken any casualties, but a big fight isn't something to ignore."

"Then let's take tomorrow off," he suggested cheerfully. "We could go on a little touristy beach date and be a loving couple."

"We have beaches in Washington," she replied.

Mason shrugged. "It's also about ten degrees colder up there now. I'm only saying, A, it's your company and we finished a job. Abuse your position a little and relax."

"We failed at a job, you mean. I know we'll be paid and it wasn't our job to authenticate the painting, but the whole thing still bugs me. The more I think about it, the angrier I get. We were played for suckers."

"There's nothing we can do about it, and if we're not blamed, there's no reason to take on the blame. That's my logic, anyway, but it's all the more reason for you to clear some of it out of your system. Maybe a little San Francisco date will give you some ideas for the wedding and honeymoon."

Alison retrieved her phone. "I suppose it wouldn't hurt if I took tomorrow off."

"If your dad can go on barbecue road trips and leave his restaurant with barely any employees for days at a time, you can leave your heavily staffed company with multiple teams for one day. Sometimes, I think you forget you don't work alone in DC anymore."

"Okay, okay." She held her hands up in front of her in mock surrender. "You've convinced me. I'll text Ava and have her schedule a flight for tomorrow night. I don't want to spend two nights here. Baby steps."

Mason snickered. "I'll take it. Half a loaf is better than none."

Alison licked her strawberry ice cream as she strolled along Pier Thirty-nine, taking in all the boats docked along the edge and the occasional boat or magical cruising through the water. Dozens of small shops filled the area, mostly food or trinket sellers, and there was something about salty air that made ice cream taste better.

Although the noon sun wouldn't be called blazing hot by most warm-blooded species' standards, the lingering chilly bite that remained in the air in Seattle was lacking in San Francisco. Alison and Mason had already shared a lovely breakfast and a silly if fun carousel ride. For a brief moment, she almost remembered what it was like years before when she didn't have worries about gangsters or dark wizards.

Mason's right. Sometimes, it's good to simply unplug and relax. I'm helping Seattle and the world, but it's not like if I take a day off everything will fall into anarchy. Dad and Mom both retired young, and they're doing okay. LA's not imploding.

With little actual ice cream left, Alison took a few big bites out of the cone to finish it.

"We could have an underwater wedding," Mason suggested with a smile. "I'm sure it'd be annoying to set all the magic up, though, but it'd be memorable."

"I don't want an underwater wedding," she replied with a laugh. "I'm not a Nereid." She watched a small boat putter past in the distance. "I keep thinking I should get a boat. Our house has a jetty, and we don't ever use it. It seems kind of wasteful."

"Why use a boat when you have a helicopter?" He shrugged. "Or when you can fly? We can both walk on water with the right spell."

"We can use it for atmosphere." She laughed and pointed to a barely discernable form leaping out of the water in the distance. "For a moment, I thought that was a dolphin, but it's clearly humanoid. I wonder if it's a wizard having a good time or a native marine species. I don't know if the Earth is ready for what it'll mean to have oceans inhabited by intelligent species. I know people believed that kind of thing back in the day, but it's been a long time."

"I don't know if Earth was truly ready for other intelligent species in general." Mason stared off into the horizon. "But everyone's adjusting. If humans have any special inherent power, it's adaptability. I think this planet will do okay even when the gates are completely open."

Alison's phone buzzed with a call.

He shook his head. "Don't answer it, A. This is supposed to be honeymoon practice."

"It might be important."

"Will the world end if you don't answer it?" He nodded at her phone. "I should have made you leave it at the hotel."

She slid her hand into her pocket and drew out the phone. "Maybe not the world, but a city could." She frowned at the caller ID. "Do I know a Raine Campbell? I feel like I should, but…"

Mason frowned a little and looked to the side as he thought about it. "The name sounds familiar, but I can't place it either."

"Well, now I'm curious." She answered the call. "Hello?"

"Is this Alison Brownstone?" a woman asked. She sounded young.

"That's me," Alison replied. "Who are you exactly?"

"Agent Raine Campbell, FBI," the caller explained.

"FBI, huh?" She took a deep breath. "You called sooner than I expected. I assume this is about the painting?"

"Yes," Raine replied. "This is about the painting, Miss Brownstone. Although San Francisco and Seattle are farther than where I usually work cases, I have some relevant expertise in the area of magical art the bureau feels will be helpful for this case. They're sending me, along with my partner, to Seattle to investigate since all our initial evidence points to the painting never leaving Seattle with your team. But I do need to officially interview you and all relevant employees as part of the investigation. I assume that's not a problem?" A hint of a challenge colored her tone.

"I'm completely prepared to fully cooperate with the FBI in this matter. Like I told the MARS people, I want this guy as much as they—and you—probably do, but I'm not back in Seattle yet and I'd like to be present before you start grilling my employees."

I don't want her to think she can push me around.

Raine considered the request in silence for several seconds. "Fair enough. I want to be clear. We don't suspect you or any of your employees of any wrongdoing, but every scrap of evidence can help. Like my mentor always said, 'Evidence leads the case.' But I know you Brownstones aren't the type to get involved in this kind of scheme."

"Oh? You've dealt with my father?"

The agent uttered a muffled snort. "I've heard of his... antics. I know he's done considerable good, but I prefer to do things a little more by the book."

Alison chuckled. "I can understand that, and I won't get

in your way. I'll have my assistant contact you so she can coordinate all the interviews. She's a wizard at this kind of thing. Well, not a wizard or even a witch, but you get the idea."

Raine laughed, a soft and friendly sound that undercut some of the tension from before. "That works. We'll try to make this quick and painless, Miss Brownstone. We'll talk soon." She ended the call.

"Why do I know the name Raine Campbell?" She stared at her phone. "I've barely dealt with the FBI, even when I was in DC. I tend to either work with PDA or local cops, but I feel like I knew her before she even called."

Mason removed his phone from his pocket and tapped it. He held it up to show her the picture. A young, pretty blonde woman in a dark suit and sunglasses stood in front of the FBI headquarters building, a wand in her hand. She still looked like a teenager in the picture, but the article was years old. The headline from the *Washington Post* article read, *A Necessary Witch? The FBI's first official magical enters the field after a tumultuous and controversial time at Quantico.*

Alison snapped her fingers. "Now I remember. It's not only that she's the first magical to openly serve in the FBI. She went to my school. She got some kind of special dispensation to join the FBI immediately after graduating because an FBI agent was there on campus also training her."

His face scrunched in confusion. "Wait. Are you talking about UCLA or the School of Necessary Magic?"

"The School of Necessary Magic," she explained. "She started the year after I graduated. I was too busy obsessing over dark wizards and bounty hunting between classes to care much about what happened there for a few years, but I now remember hearing about her. She got into almost as much trouble as I did. There was some big incident with some cult right before she graduated too, where both the kemana and Charlottesville were threatened."

"Huh. I vaguely remember when she joined the FBI, but I didn't know all that other stuff. No one blinks at magicals in those kinds of positions these days, but it was only a few years ago that they couldn't serve. It's funny how quickly things changed." Mason looked impressed. "It sounds like she was a good choice to be the FBI's first witch if she was involved in those kinds of things when she was still in school."

Alison stared at the picture. She couldn't decide if Raine looked confident or defiant. "Maybe she'll find the painting, but we'll worry about that in a few days." She smiled. "We still have a date to finish."

CHAPTER TEN

A couple of days later, Alison sat in her office across from Agent Raine Campbell. Even though the woman was only a few years younger than her, she came off as even younger. She looked much like she did in the article—an athletic young woman with long blonde hair that contrasted with her dark suit. She wasn't sure why the woman seemed so young.

Maybe it was her eyes. There was an almost innocent quality there, one unexpected for an FBI agent who had to face the corrupt world they lived in.

It's like she kept that spark I let the dark wizards crush out of me.

She had chatted only briefly with Raine's partner, Agent Clifton Hanks. Unlike his young colleague, the dark-skinned man's weathered face and graying hair suggested someone closer to retirement than his days in the FBI academy, and that made her wonder why he was still doing what appeared to be low-level field work.

Raine shifted in her chair after she'd finished her few

questions about the theft and the highway attack. They were perfunctory and without a hint of accusation.

"Thank you for taking the time and agreeing to let my partner and I interview people separately, Miss Brownstone," the agent stated. "It'll speed the process up, and I understand that this kind of thing can be tedious. The last thing we want to do is make things more obnoxious for victims, and even if you eliminated those thieves, you and your people are still victims."

"By the way, you don't need to call me Miss Brownstone," Alison responded. "It's not like I never go by it, but somehow...it feels strange coming from you." She rubbed the back of her neck.

The agent raised an eyebrow. "Why is that?"

"I don't know. Maybe because we're both Necessary Magic alumni." She shrugged. "I kind of feel a kinship there even though you started after I left."

"Fine, Alison. You can call me Raine." A ghost of a grin appeared on the woman's face. "Kinship? You're probably the single most famous person to come out of our school. Not only that, when I attended, I saw people do things like dress up as your father for Halloween."

"I'm more famous than the first open witch in the FBI?" Alison asked. "You're an actual trailblazer."

A curious glint appeared in Raine's eyes. "Yes, well, I think so anyway. The thing is, I work for a bureaucratic government law enforcement agency. If I do my job properly, I disappear into the background, especially if we stop crimes before they hurt people. We do important work, but we're also not the PDA, so we don't do some of the flashier things like worrying about Mountain Strider follow-up."

She gestured toward Alison. "And you were famous before you even graduated, after all. I might be the first witch to openly serve in the FBI, but you were the first person to be the subject of a cross-planet custody hearing, and you've racked up innumerable wins since then, too. You're practically a celebrity." There was a hint of accusation in her voice. "No, not practically a celebrity. You are a celebrity."

Is she jealous, or is this something else?

"I don't want to be a celebrity," she pointed out. "I only want to protect people. I was blessed with strong magic and running my security company is the best way I know how to use it to help people. You're in the FBI and a witch. You know how dangerous things can get out there with conspiracies not only of one world, but two."

Raine frowned slightly before she nodded. "Yes, I saw that from my first semester at the school, even if I was ignorant of it for most of my life before then. The country and the world are finally starting to get their act together about how to properly handle magicals, but the legacy of hiding the truth means there are too many criminals out there who can hide far longer than they should be able to. I was always in some kind of trouble at school from the beginning because I could never ignore someone who needed help, and that often led me to run into bad people."

"I was in more than a little trouble at school myself," Alison confirmed.

The agent smirked. "That's one way of putting it." She took a deep breath and released it slowly. "I'm sorry. I've probably come off a little rude, and I apologize. I'll admit you're not what I thought, Alison."

"And what did you think I would be?"

"I don't know. More arrogant, perhaps?" She shrugged. "I'm in law enforcement. In my perfect world, we wouldn't need to rely on bounty hunters or overly ambitious security contractors to keep people safe, but that's hypocritical on my part because like I said, I used to stick my nose into all kinds of people's problems long before I was in the FBI. None of that has anything to do with this case, though, and I should have left it outside of this office."

"I see." Alison leaned back and let some of the surprise over the revelation onto her face. "I can understand where you're coming from. Do you think there is any chance the survivors from the attack know who took the painting? While we're admitting things to one another, I'm very frustrated that my company was used, and I'm interested in making sure the people responsible are caught."

Raine frowned. "Several of the suspects are giving up everybody including their grandmothers to try to cut deals, but they don't seem to be working for anyone else. They were as surprised as you were to learn about the painting being a fake, but there is one interesting aspect to all of this that I might be able to use."

"What's that?"

She leaned forward and lowered her voice. "They had an anonymous tip. That's how they knew where to find the painting. We've verified that with a truth spell. It might not hold up in court, but it does point to the fact that they could have been used by the real mastermind." Her frown deepened into a scowl of distaste.

Alison blinked a few times. "I'm interested in all of this, but is this something you should actually tell me?"

The agent flicked her wrist dismissively. "It'll all be

announced via a press release later tonight. That much, at least."

Why is she so angry? She was calm during the interview and... Wait.

"You know who did it, don't you?" she murmured. "Or at least have a good idea. And you have some kind of history with them."

Raine's jaw tightened, and she half-closed her eyes. After several deep breaths, she opened them again and offered a forced smile. "Evidence leads the case, Alison, but instincts lead to evidence."

"Meaning what? If what you told me is true, the men who attacked my convoy were set against my people on purpose, and I'd like to know who was responsible. I need to know who targeted me." She kept her voice calm even as her heart sped up.

Raine shook her head. "This has nothing to do with you other than the fact that you were unlucky enough to be hired for security. Those thieves were nothing more than a distraction. The person responsible—or, at least, the person I believe is responsible, loves that kind of tactic and has often used it before. I think he enjoys using people like chess pieces—the more risk to their lives, the better for his entertainment. Some people grow ancient and find wisdom they want to share. Others became decadent." Her hand clenched into a fist and she shook it. "Human law was designed around human limits, including lifespans and magical limitations. It needs to change, but that's still ongoing. Now, Oricerans are here too, and most simply try to make their way like any human, but there's no such thing as a race that is all good and all bad. And when you live longer than a human, you have an opportunity for much more evil."

Alison narrowed her eyes. "It's an Oriceran behind the theft?"

"I believe so. A gnome collector of...many things—people, art, and artifacts. He goes by the name Mr. Blackthorn on Earth. He's a mysterious and dangerous figure in the art underworld." Raine unclenched her hand and lowered it to her lap, her face red. "Blackthorn has zero compunctions about hurting or killing people to get what he wants." Her nostrils flared.

"He hurt someone close to you, didn't he?" she asked, her voice almost a whisper.

The agent averted her eyes. "I ran into him a couple of times at the beginning of my career when I was fresh out of the Academy. He taught me that a few adventures at the School of Necessary Magic didn't mean I would always be able to protect the people who needed it most. So, yes, if you're asking if this is personal, it's personal. But that doesn't change the fact he's a criminal and I believe he's involved."

"Because of instincts?" Alison shrugged. "I've let them lead me down the wrong path a few times."

Raine scoffed and nodded. "That's the trick, isn't it? You need to trust your gut sometimes when the evidence isn't there, but bias can point you in the wrong direction. I have to collect the evidence, and he's good at hiding from law enforcement. He always has been." She chuckled quietly. "I don't know why I'm telling you all this. I barely know you. I'm sorry."

"Don't be." She offered a soft smile. "I think we have a

natural bond because we're both members of an exclusive club."

Raine's eyes widened. "We are?" Her gaze darted to the side for the moment. She followed it but she wasn't sure what the woman was looking at other than her empty hand.

She nodded. "Yeah, we're both members of the exclusive School of Necessary Magic Troublemakers' Club."

"Oh. I see." The woman laughed and some of the tension eased from her eyes. "That's true." She took a deep breath and stood. "I'm sorry. I'm taking up your time with my personal obsessions. I'm glad none of your people were hurt, and I promise you, if Blackthorn was involved in leaking the information, I'll add that to the list of charges so he can rot that much longer in an Ultramax." She extended her hand. "Thanks again for meeting with me and offering both your own time and that of your staff."

Alison gave her hand a firm shake. "Anything I can do to help the FBI."

"My partner and I will stick around Seattle for a few days as we continue our follow-ups," Raine explained. "I'll contact you if we need anything else, but I don't anticipate it. It was nice to meet you, Alison."

"Nice to meet you, too, Raine."

The blonde agent gave her a final smile before she left the office.

Alison frowned as she considered Raine. The young FBI agent seemed earnest, but she was law enforcement and bound by their procedures, policies, and bureaucracy, exactly as Agent Latherby was bound by similar restrictions at the PDA.

If there is some deadly gnome collector hanging out around here, he's not only a threat to me if he points criminal gangs at people. What if a less powerful security team had guarded the fake painting? And even if he's not involved, he still sounds like bad news.

She nodded decisively. It wouldn't hurt to at least check into Mr. Blackthorn.

CHAPTER ELEVEN

The following night, Alison sat at Vincent's table at the True Portal. The info broker had graduated to new levels of sartorial crime with his bright cyan leisure suit. Sometimes, she wondered if he simply messed with people—or maybe only her. The brief period of him shifting toward something more reasonable had given way in recent months to the painful outfits. Still, that didn't change the fact that he was one of her best sources of information in Seattle.

She couldn't let the theft of the painting go, even though MARS publicly praised her company's valiant efforts and made it clear the loss wasn't their fault. Raine's revelation that some Oriceran criminal mastermind might be behind the whole thing only fed her obsession.

Maybe I'm more arrogant than Raine thinks. I don't like the idea of people pulling stunts in my city like stealing two-billion-dollar paintings.

"I live to serve, Dark Princess," Vincent said dryly, lifted his apple martini to his lips, and took a sip. "Although it's been a while since you've come knocking. I thought we had a special relationship now."

She scoffed. "I saved your ass. That doesn't mean we're friends. Let's be clear about that."

"But I'm ever so grateful." He grinned and bowed over one arm. "And you're here, which means you still find what I have to offer useful, and that's all I strive to be. Useful people will always outlast people you merely like. Of course, if being useful earns me money and the occasional protection of a certain Drow princess, it's not like I'll complain."

It's almost a relief that he is as slimy as ever. I don't think I could handle it if he actually turned into a nice guy.

"I haven't needed your help lately," she explained. "And I assume if a serious threat turned up, you would at least let me know, even if you wanted a finder's fee."

"You might assume too much." Vincent set his glass down. "But there's nothing that's really come up that I think you would be all that interested in."

She glanced at the small number of guards scattered around nearby tables. Vincent's paranoia from last month was now long gone with the defeat of the men who had hunted him.

"Really?" Alison leaned forward. "Nothing I would be all that interested in, especially in the context of a missing magical painting."

"Do you have something to say?"

Time to roll the dice.

"You're telling me Mr. Blackthorn isn't in town?" she asked. "I can understand if you don't know whether he was involved in the theft, but if he's in town, I think that's important enough to pass along to me."

Vincent's mouth twitched, but he kept his placid smile despite the obvious surprise in his eyes. "Mr. Blackthorn, you say?"

"The gnome," she clarified. "In case you wondered if I was talking about anyone else. I have reason to believe he was behind the theft of the da Vinci, and if he was conveniently in the area, that would only point more to him. You don't have to be a detective to reach that conclusion."

The information broker licked his lips. "But that's not your problem anymore. I heard about it on the news. They said it was an inside job and you had to fight off a team of thieving wizards for no reason. It's all in the FBI's hands now so why do you care?"

Alison snickered. "I bet you don't volunteer information directly to law enforcement. That's why I care."

He shrugged. "A man has to have at least some standards, and as you recently learned, the last time I offered major information to the authorities, it turned out badly for me. Cops, whether feds or not, are paid well to investigate things, so they can do it without my help. Besides, they're always cheap bastards." He grunted.

"I'm not cheap," she declared. "And I want to know about Blackthorn."

"Come on, Dark Princess. Why go looking for trouble that has nothing to do with you? What does it accomplish? You have the government hunting the guy, so why do you need to?"

She glared at him. "Maybe I should have let those guys get to you if this is how it will go down."

He grimaced and placed a hand over his chest. "Ouch. I'm truly wounded."

"I'm not asking you to fight the guy. I'm only asking for information and I'm willing to pay a premium." Alison smacked her hand on the table. "So give me the damned information already."

The guards bolted from their seats, their hands already in their jackets.

Vincent threw up a hand to stop them and shook his head. He didn't bother to speak, not that they would be able to hear him outside the silence spell surrounding his table. They sank back into their seats and scowled at her.

She ignored them and fixed her attention on the man opposite her. "You obviously know something. A better strategy would have been to deny that you ever heard of him."

He chuckled. "Then I would look like an incompetent idiot. I'm willing to take threats all day before I look like an idiot." He scratched his chin. "But since you mentioned a premium, I might have remembered a few more things about our gnome friend."

"And I did save your life from hitmen," Alison pointed out. "Just throwing that out there."

"That you did." He nodded. "Here's the thing, Mr. Blackthorn doesn't normally operate in the Pacific Northwest. I don't know why that is. I've heard rumors it has something to do with the destruction of the kemana, but word has reached me that he made some recent moves in Seattle."

"Involving the da Vinci?"

Vincent shrugged. "Maybe. I don't know. Mr. Blackthorn isn't the kind of gnome you want noticing you, so I've tried to ignore whatever he's up to. Even asking the wrong kind of questions can get you noticed. I talked to a few people, and that was good enough for me."

"That's all you have? He might be in the area doing mysterious things?" She rolled her eyes. "Give me something useful, not pointless rumors."

He locked eyes with her for a moment before he nodded. "Okay, I happen to have an address of a private club. It's kind of an underground establishment that certain magicals with dubious intentions use. Mr. Blackthorn's been seen there on occasion, and I heard he's been a regular there over the last few days."

Alison nodded. "That's better. What's the club like?"

"I don't know." The broker frowned and smoothed his lapels. "I've never been there."

She gave him an incredulous look. "You've never been to a club filled with the movers and shakers of the underworld? I find that hard to believe."

"Sometimes, the best way to not end up in trouble is to never go near it," he pointed out. "Even if there might be rewards. I don't know a lot about the club but considering some of the names associated with it, I'm sure it's the kind of place where an information broker of strained but not completely tainted morality wouldn't want to go."

"You're telling me there's some depraved club for magicals in Seattle and you're only letting me know now?" She growled her irritation.

Vincent shook his head. "It's not in Seattle, though. I don't actually know where it is."

"You told me you had the address." Alison scrubbed a

hand down her face. "Are you messing with me now? I'm not in the mood."

"Calm down, Dark Princess." He picked up his martini and took another sip. "I know where a gateway leading to it is. There's an alley at the address. From what I understand, no one can get to the club without taking one of the established gateways. If you try to portal to it directly, it'll always fail. I don't know if anyone other than the owners really know where the club is. It could be anywhere on Earth or Oriceran. I'm a specialist in information about things happening in Seattle, and so no, I don't feel I have to tell you about every hidden den out there that might exist somewhere on both planets. Besides, I only learned about the gateway recently, and I didn't even have the card you need to activate it until a few days ago—which I only fell into because of luck. I'm willing to give you the card, but that'll cost you, too."

She snorted. "Of course it will. Aren't you the greedy one?"

"A man has to be rewarded for his efforts and risks, but I can't guarantee anything." Vincent frowned at her. "All I know is that Blackthorn's been seen at the club recently, and that it might have something to do with things happening in Seattle, but I make no guarantees. Besides, I still think you might not want to be involved in this. You can't take on the entire world, and if you stir the pot against guys not even from Seattle, you might give people the wrong idea."

"Oh?" Alison folded her arms over her chest. "And what idea is that? I've gone after numerous people outside of Seattle before."

"But you've generally let people feel that if they stayed out of your way, they would be fine." He clucked his tongue. "And when you've done most things outside of the city, it's because you've been hired by someone—or someone made a mistake and gave you a reason to come after them. You're strong enough to control this city, but are you strong enough to take on two worlds' worth of trouble?"

She rolled her eyes. "This isn't about taking everyone on. This is about checking on one particular gnome who is more likely than not to have caused me trouble. I think if anyone thinks that translates into open season on me, they should consult with the Seventh Order and ask how that worked out for them."

Vincent laughed. "You don't give up, do you? I might have to get a new job if you keep things up. This city might end up as boring as LA."

"There's still crime in LA," she observed.

"Far less than there should be for a city that size." He gulped the rest of his drink. "Fine. You win. I'll give you the card and the address, but if anyone comes asking, I'll deny it. And you'd better make sure that if Blackthorn's there, you eliminate him."

"Why?" Alison asked. "Do you think he's that much of a monster?"

"No." He shook his head. "I don't want him to target me."

CHAPTER TWELVE

Somebody kill me now.

Alison groaned as she strolled down the street toward the address, Mason smiling beside her. Hana had loaned her six-inch heels, a red micro-skirt, and a halter top. She wasn't sure if the club would question too many spells, so she'd gone with a red wig and green contacts rather than relying on illusion magic. It had seemed pointless to question why Ava conveniently had a disguise kit in her desk but now, a freckled woman with full cheeks walked on the arm of a bearded man in a suit. They presumed no one would question Mason's wand, but he still kept it concealed in his jacket.

"I feel ridiculous," she muttered. "I look ridiculous. I look like I should take you to the kind of hotel that charges by the hour."

"You look fine, Beatrice," he replied with a grin.

"I never agreed to that name," she retorted.

"Sure thing, B." He winked.

"Don't have too much fun." She tightened her grip on

the clutch in her left hand. The card they needed lay inside. "We should have simply busted in there and demanded to see Blackthorn."

"A little subterfuge never hurts," Mason suggested. "He might not even be there. Vincent said he'd been there, but we can't be sure he still is. If we do this the traditional Brownstone way, we might blow our chance of catching him. Although it might help if we knew what Blackthorn actually looked like."

"Even the FBI doesn't have a picture of him. I had Ava check." Alison shrugged. "I guess you have a point. I don't know why I've let this get under my skin so much."

"Substitution," he responded.

"What?"

"It's a substitute for the Tapestry," he suggested. "It's a problem you can solve without waiting for them to make their next move."

She pondered that before she replied with a nod. "Okay. Maybe."

They turned the corner and walked another few yards before they stopped in front of an otherwise nondescript empty alley. A yard away, she'd felt nothing, but now that she stood in front of it, magic saturated the area.

"It looks like we're here," Mason commented and scrutinized the area with a frown.

Alison nodded. "It looks like it." She opened the clutch and withdrew the white card from Vincent. Several complicated glyphs were inscribed on its face. She rubbed her thumb over them. The alleyway darkened, the shadows crawling to smother all the light.

"That's not creepy at all," her boyfriend muttered.

"At least we know we're in the right place." She tightened her hold on his arm, not sure if the gateway was an area teleport. They took slow, deliberate steps until the all-encompassing shadow surrounded them. The air turned chilly.

She rubbed her shoulders. "I don't like this. It's like we're going to the World in Between."

"That would be impressive," he whispered.

The shadows disappeared and the alley was gone, replaced by a large but dim circular room. A floral scent lingered in the air, carried by the smoke rising from incense in pyramidal clay containers resting on dark wooden tables filling the space over a thick, lush dark-green carpet. Dull white light orbs hovered above the tables and cast enough light to fight off the darkness but left sufficient shadows that it was difficult to make out anyone's features from a distance.

The couple stood in front of a large black door with a crystal knob. It matched a dozen others spread out evenly along the walls.

How many hidden places like this are there in the two worlds?

Dozens of people from different species filled the room. Elves, gnomes, and dwarves were prominent among them, but others included a table of nichts, their leathery wings folded behind their backs. Four mantis-like creatures with dark-red solid eyes stood around a table and chittered among themselves. Alison couldn't even guess the species. A raised stage filled one side of the room, but no one stood on it and it remained unlit. There were no obvious bouncers, and no one even glanced at them. Light flute music filled the room from no discernable source.

"I'm a little underdressed," she murmured and inclined her head slightly toward a Gray Elf in a robe embroidered with silver and gold sigils.

"You're fine, B," Mason replied, a grin still on his face.

Why do I have the feeling he'll use that nickname for weeks?

He tugged on her arm and led her toward an empty table near the stage that was surrounded by a few others, equally empty. He stepped away from her and pulled out her chair. She sat and realized the table gave her a strategic view of the entire room.

Good choice.

After he sat, she cast a silence spell around the table. Given the sheer level of magic that permeated the club, she doubted anyone would take particular notice. She couldn't hear the seven dwarves clustered around two tables having what appeared to be an animated discussion, which made her think they were already using similar magic. A few murmurs filled the air, but there wasn't enough background noise to account for all the people in the room.

I could have used a disguise spell after all. Live and learn.

Mason looked around. "Now what?"

"We find Mr. Blackthorn," she replied. "And we ask him a few pointed questions."

"But we don't know what he looks like," he reminded her. "And there are several gnomes in here. Will we simply go up to each of them and ask, 'Hey, are you the mysterious Mr. Blackthorn and did you steal the painting?'"

Alison shrugged. "If it comes down to it, yes. I put on this ridiculous disguise, so I might as well make use of it."

She surveyed the room again, but no one looked at her. "This isn't working out the way we planned. I was supposed to look different enough that no one would recognize me without using a spell but would still draw attention, but no one cares. Maybe it's too dim to notice."

"Don't worry. I still think you're hot." He winked infuriatingly. "You don't need bright lights to appreciate that."

"I suppose we can ask if a waiter comes." She took a deep breath. Her heart was beating harder than she expected, considering that they hadn't run into any trouble yet.

I'm too much of a Brownstone in the end. We should have brought Hana to sneak around and flirt. I want to give up and give a big speech about how Blackthorn should merely surrender.

She frowned.

Wait. Did Hana just convince me this outfit would work because she wanted to see me in it? She did seem way too eager to take pictures. That sneaky fox.

"Remember," Mason whispered despite the silence spell, "we're only here for information. We're not here to confront anyone. The two of us are tough, but I don't think we can win against everyone in this room."

"We don't have to." Alison turned her head from side to side and tried not to stare as her gaze searched for someone who might be Blackthorn. "Just because everyone's in this club doesn't mean they're all friends. Still, I have to admit, it's not as disgusting as I thought it would be."

"They probably only plan the nasty things here," he observed. "Think about the corrupt elites throughout history who might have hung out in places like this while they devised ways to screw other people over."

She sighed. Vincent had suggested that the people who frequented the club were far worse than the run-of-the-mill criminals and scum she dealt with in Seattle.

"I can't—" She inclined her head in the direction of an approaching bald gnome who wore a white suit and matching bowtie. "Someone's finally paying attention."

They waited in silence and stared at him as he maneuvered slowly through the tables. He nodded to various patrons along the way and received smiles and greetings in return.

The gnome finally arrived at their table. He stopped a few feet away and appraised them before he took a few more steps forward and inside her anti-sound bubble.

"I've been alive for a long time," he explained. "And I've seen wonders on both this planet and Oriceran, but even I find myself surprised at this situation." He stared at Alison, his lips curled in amusement. His eyes didn't roam over her body. Instead, he stared directly into her eyes.

"What's the big surprise?" Alison asked.

"That Alison Brownstone would be bold enough to stroll into this club with only one wizard on her arm." The gnome chuckled darkly. "Perhaps, Dark Princess, your arrogance is beginning to catch up with you. You're powerful, yes, but you're not immortal."

"I'm not Alison Brownstone," she insisted. "I don't even look anything like her. Hello? Redhead here."

The gnome reached up, and she flexed her fingers, ready to summon a shadow blade. He didn't cast a spell but instead, continued to move his fingers toward his left eye. He tapped it, and Alison winced.

"It's an artifact," he explained. "I always see the true form of what I look at. Magic, technology, simple disguises...none work on me. After all, when you're as interested in collecting things as I am, it's important to be able to verify that you aren't being tricked, and it helps with that."

"Blackthorn," Alison spat and gritted her teeth.

He nodded. "Yes, I'm Mr. Blackthorn." He smiled at her, but it didn't reach his eyes. "And to what do I owe the pleasure of this visit? I'm curious how you even got in here, but sometimes, mysteries are entertaining, so I'll settle for the answer to the first question."

"Where is it?" she demanded.

Mason kept his hand inside his jacket, hovering over his wand. He hadn't bothered to bring a gun since they weren't sure if they would have been ejected if they brought an actual weapon.

"Where is what?" Blackthorn asked.

"*Axis Omnium Mundos*," she replied. "I've been told you might have been behind its theft. Or will you deny it?"

"I see." The gnome looked down and sighed. "I could deny it, but what's the point? You went through all the trouble to track me and gain access to this place, so I doubt you'll take my word for it. Besides, what's the point of collecting something if you can't brag about owning it? Yes, I have the painting. I look forward to years of unlocking its secret."

"And you talk about me being arrogant." She glared at him. "You have to give it back."

Blackthorn chuckled. "Why ever would I do that?"

Mason frowned. "A, something's wrong. Look around."

Half the patrons had risen and made their way to one of the doors. The seven dwarves practically sprinted while others, such as the Arpaks, strolled out, their heads held high. Alison couldn't read their faces in the dim lighting.

Do they know who I am? Or are they more worried about him? It's time to get ready.

"That's fine by me. It means less collateral damage if something happens." Alison shrugged and kicked her heels off before she turned back to the gnome. "I've heard a lot about how you're not the nicest gnome, Blackthorn, but I'm not here to arrest you, even if you have a class-five bounty on you."

Mason blinked. "He does?"

She nodded. "I was curious, so I checked. It's rare to have a bounty on someone they don't even have a good description for, but I'm not interested in the money anyway. I'm not even interested in him directly."

Blackthorn sighed. "Only class-five? I'm almost insulted. But if you're not here for the bounty, why bother coming at all? It's my understanding that you weren't even blamed for the incident."

"No, MARS didn't blame me, but that doesn't change the fact that you stole a two-billion-dollar painting out from under my nose—technically, if not actually." She snorted her disgust. "And, quite frankly, it shouldn't be with you. It should be with MARS."

"The people who couldn't protect it? That sounds dubious if you ask me, but I do admit a bias in this matter."

"They couldn't protect it from you," she insisted. "That's a little different."

The gnome wagged a short finger and clucked his tongue. "A man who worked for MARS saw an opportunity, and I helped facilitate it. Nothing more than that."

"And you didn't happen to help leak the news and transport plan to encourage a gang of wizards to attack us and draw off suspicion?" She scoffed.

Mason continued to look around the room at the departing crowd and his frown deepened. His attention lingered on the people who remained seated.

"Do you really want that painting so badly, Brownstone?" Blackthorn asked, a slight sneer on his face.

"Yes." Alison stood. It wasn't hard for a human to tower over a gnome, but he didn't look intimidated, only more amused at the action.

"I can give you the painting," he announced. "Since you went through all this trouble."

"You can?" both Alison and Mason asked simultaneously.

The gnome nodded. "I can be reasonable. No matter what you think of my methods, I'm first and foremost a collector. I don't harbor any pointless desires to harm people for the sake of harming them. I'm not a thug."

"Killing and hurting people is still a crime." She gestured around the room. "Just because you're doing it the name of your stupid collection doesn't change that, but whatever. I don't care. You can give me the painting, and I'll turn it over to the feds, and they can discuss things with MARS from there. You can wander off and stay out of Seattle."

"I'll need something in return," Blackthorn clarified, a huge grin on his face. "It's only fair."

Mason grunted but didn't say anything.

"What?" she asked.

Blackthorn spread his hands in front of him. "I'll even give you a little discount. Give me a billion dollars, and I'll give you the painting."

She stared at him, her mind reeling and her heart at a gallop. He couldn't have possibly said what she had heard.

"What?" she repeated. "Did you—"

"I want a billion dollars," he insisted. "That's a reasonable price."

Alison took a few deep breaths and released them slowly. "You know what? Who cares? I think that the world would be better off if I knocked you out and dragged you to the FBI. I can consider it a favor for a fellow School of Necessary Magic alumnus. Raine's very eager to meet you face to face."

The gnome's mouth twisted into a sneer. "Agent Campbell?" He growled with menace. "That indefatigable witch has hounded me for far too long. I should have killed her years ago." He snapped his fingers and teleported several yards away in an instant. A wave of magic radiated from him, and the flute music cut off before Alison's silence bubble surrounded them once again.

Quick anti-magic. Impressive.

"What are you doing?" Alison asked and kept any hint of concern out of her voice. She didn't want him to think he scared her.

All the remaining patrons—a mixture of elves, wizards, and witches—stood from their tables. The latter two groups had their wands out and hungry looks in their eyes. The mantis creatures from before also remained.

Mason grasped his wand and clenched his jaw.

She summoned a shield. "You don't want to do this, Blackthorn. I'll give you one last chance to surrender."

Okay, this didn't go down the way I expected. Oh, well. Sometimes, it's good to have a little therapeutic exercise.

"I refuse to deal with any friend of Agent Campbell!" he shouted. "And now, I'll send her another message about what happens to those who oppose me. It's time to die, Brownstone."

CHAPTER THIRTEEN

A shadow blade extended when Alison raised her hand and released shadow magic into it. "You really, really don't want to do this, Blackthorn."

Mason rushed through a shield spell with concern as he watched the surrounding magicals gather.

The air shimmered in front of the gnome. "Did you really think you could come to my place and threaten me, Brownstone?"

"Your place?" She layered another shield. While she didn't want to fight, that didn't mean she wouldn't prepare.

Vincent left out a few key details about this club. I guess it doesn't matter now.

"Of course." Blackthorn sneered. "Why would I spend time in a location I don't control?" He raised his right hand and a gold ring covered in dozens of small diamonds appeared. "But if you kiss my ring and ask for forgiveness, I'll forgive you."

"How magnanimous," she muttered. "But what happened to killing me?"

Mason finished a few more enhancement spells. Every second the fight delayed was an additional advantage for the Brownstone duo.

His lackeys haven't shielded up. Do they know something I don't know?

"I don't want to risk unnecessary damage to my club," the gnome explained. "You can't imagine the effort and time required to stabilize the many enchantments that go into this place." For all his sneering condescension, he continued to walk steadily backward until he stood among some of his men.

"I won't kiss your ring," she replied and began to shunt magic into her legs and feet. "I'll defeat you."

Blackthorn shook his head. "A pity. You had potential." He snapped his fingers. "Kill them but try to not damage her face too much. I want it for my collection."

"That's gross." Alison released her pooled magic and launched upward. She flew not toward Blackthorn and the small number of elves and wizards around him but chose a larger force of adversaries off to his side. They shouted and pointed their wands, but their sluggish reactions and wide eyes proved that they weren't ready.

Mason took advantage of the confusion to hurtle forward and moved at almost a blur as he vaulted over tables into the center of the line.

Her blade stabbed through the head of a wizard. He dropped, and she ducked as a nearby witch and wizard on opposite sides blasted fireballs toward her. The deadly flames passed over her and the attackers exchanged shots instead. They both screamed and fell, their chests scorched.

This is the problem with thugs. All that power, but they're worthless when they come up against someone with actual training. They should have shielded up when they had the chance.

She jabbed backward without turning her head and pierced the chest of a scowling Wood Elf who had raised his hand for a spell.

Mason launched from a table and dropkicked a wizard with the full momentum of his charge. The man catapulted with a scream and a loud crunch. The life wizard pushed off the ground before he landed fully and bounded a little farther ahead before he stopped.

A spinning chain materialized and careened toward him, but he matched its rotation, caught it, and flung it at a nearby witch. The hard metal wound around her, and she fell with a yelp as her wand was dislodged from her hand.

Alison sliced another witch's wand before she struck her in the chest with a light bolt. Most of the enemies close by fled the area and kicked tables over while they finally cast shield spells.

So you finally realized it wouldn't be an easy win, huh?

The mantis men stood several yards away, their carapaces now glowing a dull scarlet, but they didn't move toward either Alison or Mason.

A Light Elf nearby grinned and a gleaming sword of pure white appeared in his hand. "I'll enjoy killing you, Brownstone. All you Drow are so arrogant."

She rolled her eyes. "The Fixer and King Oriceran would be ashamed of you."

The elf thrust at her with his blade. She parried with her own and a slight flash sizzled when the energy blades met. The Light Elf stabbed at her shoulder and struck her shield, but the attack only forced her back with a slight sting.

There's tremendous power in that thing. If I weren't shielded, I'd probably be dead.

A few other elves and wizards regained their courage and moved closer to circle her. A riot of magical bolts accompanied by fireballs pounded against her sides and back, straining her shields, and the stings built to actual pain. The enemies might be cautious enough not to fire blindly and hit their ally, but that left them numerous target angles.

A fireball exploded against her back, and she hissed in pain when it scorched her. The warning told her that her shields were failing.

And I'm in a stupid halter top. Great.

Mason flung an unconscious wizard toward the enemies behind her. They panicked and launched a barrage against their friend.

"This is ridiculous," Blackthorn shouted. "Kill them already! Everyone will get a bonus, but whoever strikes the final blow will get a major reward."

The Light Elf rushed forward for another hasty attempt. Alison blocked the blow and thrust out her free arm to conjure a shadow crescent at point-blank range. The magic struck the elf's shield, and he staggered. She slashed her blade from side to side so he had no time to recover.

Mason's follow-up charge into the enemies divided their attention. His punches and kicks might not actually kill the now shielded foes, but the bodies he hurled with the force of his attacks made it difficult for the other guards to attack with impunity.

Blackthorn marched over to the all but immobile mantis men, shook his head, and muttered under his breath. He murmured something to them.

Alison's shadow blade finished its deadly work and ripped through the Light Elf's shield. Her blade plunged through his chest, and the elf blinked several times, utter shock on his face. She yanked the weapon out and twirled while she fired light bolts to suppress the attackers who hadn't been thrown around by Mason. Several ducked.

With her immediate foes defeated, she strengthened her shields and took a few deep breaths. The burns on her back continued to throb, but she did her best to ignore them. She'd felt a lot worse.

Four wizards stood quickly, ready to deliver a magical volley at Mason. He staggered when their simultaneous bolts and fireballs scorched his jacket.

Alison sprinted forward and summoned a second blade. She yelled, and two of the wizards turned in time for her to stab at one. His defenses held for the initial attack, but a quick flurry soon introduced her blades to his neck.

Mason took the opportunity to launch one of the nearby men upward with a magically charged uppercut. The man crashed through the ceiling and the lower half of his body hung in the darkness like a twisted chandelier.

She released her blades and thrust her palm out to deliver a blindingly bright light bolt directly into another wizard. Her attack seared through his already weakened shield, and he spun a few times before he collapsed and the acrid smell of his burnt flesh filled the air.

Mason pounded away at an enemy, his fists a blur. The

thin shield of magic protecting the man failed, and the life wizard's fist hammered into his face with the force of a vehicle collision.

The Brownstone duo stood back to back, their breathing ragged. The dead and wounded surrounded them.

Damn. If we had Drysi and Hana, we would have annihilated them without even breaking a sweat.

Blackthorn remained near the mantis men.

What the hell?

Alison expected a face twisted in irritation and anger, not a gnome who smirked in amusement. She narrowed her eyes before she whispered a healing spell to take care of her burns. Mason hastily cast his own.

"You've lost, Blackthorn," she challenged. "Unless those four…uh, whatever they are, happen to be way, way more powerful than your other goons, you're done. Or will you run? Go ahead, but you'll lose your little clubhouse."

"I have no intention of running." The gnome flicked his wrist dismissively. "I'll admit you've done better than I expected, but that doesn't change the fact you won't survive this."

Six of the doors on the other side of the room flung open, and mantis men poured out like angry bees protecting their hive.

Alison couldn't help but wonder if a portal had opened when she entered from the alley. A more serious concern pushed out the stray thought.

"What the hell?" She pushed more energy into her shields. "Who the hell are these guys?"

"It's amazing who you run into when you wander

around underground," Blackthorn replied. "It's something Earth people—even magicals—don't properly appreciate. Not every race on Oriceran feels a need to interact much with the others. Some barely deal with those outside their environment. There's a balance there lacking on Earth." He nodded at one of the mantis men closest to him. "The Ilzic are very loyal when you compensate them properly. I'll need your head for my collection, but they don't get to feast much on someone truly powerful. There are too many rules on Oriceran for them to feast on what they prefer, but a taste of you will be like ambrosia to them."

She grimaced. "No thanks. I think I'd leave a bad aftertaste."

Every new arrival glowed the same color as the four originals and the combined effect gave the entire room a sinister red glow.

"Damn it, A," Mason muttered. "That's a lot of hungry bugs."

The doors closed to leave dozens of the creatures that all chittered and scraped their clawed hands over one another.

"You had your chance, Brownstone," Blackthorn stated with a sneer. "You should have understood who you were dealing with."

Another door flung open on the opposite side of the room.

Alison gritted her teeth.

More reinforcements?

A figure in gray power armor rushed through, FBI RRAET stenciled over the chest and a rifle in hand. A rapid response anti-enhanced threat team had miraculously arrived. Another agent followed, then another. Within moments, six of the team in power armor stood spread out along the wall, their rifles aimed and ready.

Blackthorn frowned, but his forces seemed undeterred.

Two agents walked in a few seconds later—Raine and her partner Agent Hanks. There was a slight shimmer around them, and they both wore FBI ballistic vests. Raine had her wand out, but Agent Hanks held a submachine gun.

The gnome's jaw dropped. "Impossible."

Raine smiled. "Mr. Blackthorn, you're under arrest." She looked meaningfully at the Ilzic. "The rest of you will stand down. I'm Agent Raine Campbell of the FBI, and anyone who aids Mr. Blackthorn can be charged as an accomplice to any number of his crimes."

The Ilzic chittered in response, but it was nothing intelligible in English. Alison wondered if they were incapable of translation magic or simply didn't care

The agent surveyed the room before she turned to Alison. "You've been busy."

She shrugged. "I got too curious for my own good, and then Blackthorn tried to make me kiss his ring so I decided I wanted to kick his ass."

"I understand that. I have the same problem." Raine laughed. "With the curiosity, not the ring kissing."

"Enough!" the gnome shrieked. He cut through the air with hand and all the doors vanished. "Do you children think you can survive against me? You're nothing but more meat for the Ilzic. Do you think you can win? Their claws are excellent at tearing through magical shields. In the long-distant past, when Oriceran was peaceful, they were sought out as valuable mercenaries and now, you'll learn why."

Raine and Alison exchanged glances and turned toward Mr. Blackthorn, hungry smiles on their faces. Agent Hanks didn't smile, but he didn't frown either.

"You got sloppy, Blackthorn," Raine replied calmly. "You thought you would always be one step ahead of me, but you didn't wipe your trail this time. Maybe grabbing the painting went to your head, but the fact that I'm here and Alison Brownstone is here is proof enough of that. Why don't you simply surrender and make this easy on all of us?"

"It's time to end this farce." Mr. Blackthorn raised his arm and sliced his hand downward. The Ilzic surged forward.

CHAPTER FOURTEEN

The insectoid horde swept toward the FBI, Alison, and Mason. Agent Hanks' gun and the rifles of the RRAET came to life. Their muzzle flashes lit up the shadowed room. Bullets ripped through the first few attackers. Blue blood erupted from their wounds, and they collapsed with a screech and their scarlet glow faded.

The remaining Ilzic hesitated for a moment, chittering and hissing.

They must have had some kind of magic layer they thought would protect them, but it doesn't do much to stop rifles with anti-magic bullets.

Raine shouted a spell. Several tables flipped onto their side and slid together to form a natural barrier high enough to inconvenience the Ilzic but still low enough to fire over. Her partner raised his weapon and licked his lips.

Alison took a few steps back and shoved her hands together. She funneled energy into a growing white-blue orb. Mason swung his wand in arc. Sharp spikes grew from the overturned tables.

The enemy charged again. A burst of FBI anti-magic bullets from the RRAET team and Agent Hanks shredded their resurgent front line. The next wave scrambled over the bodies of their fallen brethren and attempted to leap and climb over the wall of tables. Spikes snagged a few and slowed them, which gave the FBI team more time to annihilate them.

Raine moved her wand in an elaborate motion as she rattled off a complicated incantation. A buffeting wind blew hard in front of the tables and slowed the progress of the advancing assailants. Alison continued to feed her orb, which now crackled with power. Mason remained near her and his next spell increased the number of spikes on the tables.

Blackthorn stood at the back, his mouth set in a tight line. A thick glowing green bubble appeared around him.

Alison thrust her arms forward and released the orb. The bright ball of energy rocketed across the room and struck the center of the insectoid army. A blue-white explosion enveloped several of them and the nearby tables and the shockwave knocked others over.

The Ilzic screeched as one and the sharp sound echoed in the room. The survivors scampered back onto their four legs in an instant and the scarlet glow around them grew brighter, but only about a dozen of the original force remained.

I'll give them this. They're damned brave. Stupid, but brave.

Another attack followed, but the FBI power armor team methodically fired rapid bursts into the approaching ranks. Within twenty seconds, their guns fell silent and all the Ilzic lay motionless, bleeding out.

"It's over, Blackthorn," Raine shouted and scowled at him. "We have already traced this place's true location, and I'm sure the PDA team we have helping us will have a portal established soon enough. I order you to open the doors." She pointed at a softly chittering Ilzic lying in a pool of his own blood on the FBI side of the barricade. "We can still save them."

The gnome folded his arms and the green light of the bubble around him gave his skin a sickly cast. "I don't take orders from witches."

The RRAET team members changed their magazines and took several loud steps forward, their rifles trained on Blackthorn.

Alison shrugged. "I don't think you'll win against seven guys using anti-magic bullets, a Drow princess, a life wizard, and the FBI's first witch. There's being stubborn, and there's being a damned moron."

He rolled his eyes. "You won't get through this barrier. I could survive a nuclear blast in here." He reached into his pocket and withdrew a smooth gray stone. "I've had a long time to prepare. Do you think I believed I would never be cornered?"

The FBI team advanced until they reached the table wall. They kicked the furniture aside with their armored legs and continued toward Blackthorn. Agent Hanks remained on their flank and also aimed his weapon at the gnome.

Raine slid her wand into a loop on the side of her vest as she jogged after the other agents. "That's your big plan? You'll simply turtle up and hope we'll go away? I'm kind of disappointed, Blackthorn. I thought you would at least rant about how you would blow us up or something."

"Do you think the Ilzic are the only allies I have available?" he countered. "And I refuse to give my life to eliminate lesser creatures such as you. Honestly, you're simply not worth it."

Alison pointed at the bubble. "I could try to overwhelm it." She gestured around the scorched piles of blackened wood strewn around the room. "But it might take the whole place with it."

The doors reappeared. A couple opened, and more FBI agents rushed in—this time in suits rather than power armor—but all carried pistols or submachine guns. A few wizards advanced after them with their wands at the ready and stern looks on their faces.

"I told you the PDA would solve our little door problem," Raine said with a smile at Blackthorn. "Once we were actually able to trace this place, it was all over for you. Sure, we still have to use one of your access points, but that also means you have to use one to get out of here. Isn't that ironic? You can't escape because of the very thing you put in here to control access." She looked at Alison. "By the way, he has everyone convinced his club is hidden in some deep corner of Oriceran, but it's actually in a building in Omaha."

Alison laughed. "Omaha? Really? I have nothing against the city but it's…" She shrugged.

"It's not the city you think of when you think about hidden magical criminal lairs," Raine finished.

"Maybe he's full of crap," Agent Hanks suggested. "He's trying to bluff his way out."

Blackthorn knelt, a growing smirk on his face. "Go ahead and shoot. Or wait until my reinforcements arrive. It doesn't matter to me. You won't take me here, human."

Agent Hanks aimed the gun to the side of Blackthorn but still at the bubble. He pulled the trigger. The bullet bounced off the green energy field with a spark and clattered onto the floor. He grimaced. "I don't want to think about how much taxpayer money I wasted to test a theory."

"You children weren't prepared," the gnome crowed. "The Dark Princess of Seattle and the Necessary Witch. You've come all this way and tried so hard for nothing."

Raine sighed. "I can't believe people still call me that. That stupid article will haunt me for years."

Maybe I shouldn't mention that I read it the other day.

The agent withdrew a small silver pin from her pocket. "You know, Blackthorn, I've chased you since the beginning of my field career." She stepped toward him. The FBI agents filled in her flanks on either side.

His attention settled on the pin. "What's that?"

"I visit a good friend of mine a couple of times a year at the School of Necessary Magic," she explained. "A good gnome who works in a library."

He sniffed disdainfully. "I'm sure he wears a silly human hat, too."

"His hats are cool, actually," she insisted. "They have flowers that blow raspberries and growl." She continued toward the bubble. "He gave me something as a kind of present after I graduated from the FBI Academy, an old artifact he found a few centuries ago. He said I might find it useful someday, but I'd only ever get one use out of it."

She lifted the pin and offered the gnome a wide grin. "Do you want to guess what it does?"

"I can tell you that I don't care."

She thrust the pin into the bubble, and both disappeared in a bright flash. As she ran forward, she whipped out a pair of anti-magic cuffs. Blackthorn was on the ground seconds later, her knee in his back and her cuffs around his wrists. In a calm voice, the FBI agent recited his Miranda Rights.

He stared off into the distance, his face pinched in confusion. "I shouldn't have lost. I couldn't have lost."

Raine patted him on the head. "I guess the only question is if you'll go to an Ultramax or Trevilsom. I'm sure there are all kinds of people who want to have a chat with you on both planets, Blackthorn."

"You haven't won, girl," the gnome spat. "You have no idea of the connections I've established."

"Sure, sure." She stood and pointed to him. "Gentlemen, if you would."

The RRAET advanced. One of them yanked the prisoner to his feet. All of them aimed their weapons at him as they marched the cuffed gnome toward the reinforcements. The newly arrived wizards moved toward some of the wounded on the floor and drew out their wands to stabilize them. Mason joined them in their efforts.

Agent Hanks shouldered his weapon and smiled at his partner. "How does it feel?"

"Damned good, Clifton. Damned good." She exhaled a long, happy sigh. "I thought I'd never catch him."

Alison released her lingering defensive spells. "You

came in at a good time, so I won't complain too much, but why are you here? Did you follow me?"

Did they use me?

Raine shook her head. She tapped the letters F, B, and I in order on her vest. "I'm an FBI agent. I investigate things for a living, and like I said, he got sloppy and left a trail, but it did get easier to open the door a few minutes before we entered. I wonder if that had something to do with you annihilating half the guys in here." She flicked her wrist toward a downed wizard nearby. "You really cleaned these guys out before we showed up, and your little exploding orb helped. Like I told you before, I've always kind of been suspicious of you Brownstones, but I appreciate your help."

Alison extended her hand. "You're welcome. Anything for a fellow Necessary Magic Cardinal."

The agent shook her hand.

"If you have time tomorrow, maybe you could join me for some victory sushi," Alison suggested.

She raised an eyebrow. "Victory sushi?"

"It's kind of a Brownstone Security tradition. There's a great place in Seattle. Maneki. It's been there for over a century."

Raine looked at her partner.

Agent Hanks gave her a slight nod. "You go ahead. I'll handle the bureaucratic garbage. You'll probably talk about all the magic stuff that happened at your school anyway." He chuckled. "No offense, Miss Brownstone, but too much magic talk bores me."

"It sounds like we have a plan then," Raine agreed with a smile.

CHAPTER FIFTEEN

Alison opened her mouth and popped in a piece of salmon nigiri. She chewed slowly to savor the flavor. Mason knelt beside her at the low table in a private room at Maneki, sipping his sake. Raine and Hana sat across from the couple.

They had been eating for about fifteen minutes, mostly exchanging small talk. There was a comfortable ease in dealing with Raine, even though Alison didn't know her well. She might be an FBI agent dedicated to her job, but there was a natural warmth to her that was compelling. They might have been good friends had they gone to school together.

"I'm sorry you couldn't meet Drysi and Tahir," she said. "You would have liked them. Well, maybe Drysi."

Hana laughed. "Ouch."

"You know Tahir. He can be...prickly with new people."

"True enough, but I've tamed him." The fox grinned.

Alison didn't want to admit to Raine that both missing team members had made it very clear they didn't want to spend their evening with an overly earnest FBI agent who might be less tolerant of their backgrounds than their employer. The infomancer also insisted that someone needed to watch Omni, just in case, but she didn't buy that excuse. He was anti-social on a good day, so there was no reason to press him on the matter.

The red-faced Hana lifted her sake cup and gulped the liquor. "Screw the party-poopers. More sushi and sake for us! They don't know what they're missing. There's nothing better than victory sushi when you didn't even have to do anything to earn it."

Raine avoided the sake but had already eaten several pieces of sushi. She stared at Hana for a moment before she averted her eyes.

The other woman leaned toward her, suspicion in her eyes. "What? Do I have rice on my face?"

"No, but..." The agent shook her head. "Nothing. I went to school with a kitsune, and I was thinking about how you remind me of her in some ways, but you're different in so many others. You two look nothing alike, so maybe it's weird that I even think that way, but she also can be...colorful."

Hana wagged her finger. "Kitsune aren't the same as nine-tailed foxes. I know the human myths have depicted them as the same, but in the real world, even though many of their kind bred with my kind, we're distinct species. I'm a shapeshifter, not a trickster magical." Her glowing tails appeared, and her eyes turned vulpine. "This is natural for me, not a spell."

"That's very pretty," Raine responded tentatively.

"Thank you." She looked at her boss. "How come you never say my tails are pretty?"

Alison shrugged. "I'll try to do that going forward."

Hana gave her a thumbs-up. "A little appreciation goes a long way."

"And I understand that you're different from a kitsune," Raine continued. She picked up her cup of tea and took a sip. "When I was in school, I loved the library, and I researched all that back then. I've met several kitsunes, but I never had the opportunity to actually meet a nine-tailed fox until now."

The fox nodded with a serene look. Her eyes returned to brown, and her tails vanished. "There aren't many of us in America, but maybe someday, one will go to that school."

"I hope she is involved in less trouble than we were. Most of that was my fault, though, not my kitsune friend's. Although she did once accidently bring cupcakes to life." A wistful smile appeared on Raine's face.

Mason finished a rice ball before he looked from Alison to Raine. "Why do I feel like I would have been in nothing but trouble if I had gone to your school? You were supposed to be learning there, but you mostly seemed to have run around getting involved in mischief."

"Most people stayed out of trouble," Alison commented. "And we learned, too. The dark wizard attack crap changed everything for everyone, but it wasn't like the average student ran into the messes I did along with my friends. We were unusual, even at a school filled with magicals."

"So were we," Raine replied. "They even gave us a name

—the FBI Trouble Squad." Her fingers danced along the silver tray holding the sushi for a moment before she selected a salmon roll. "I dragged most of my friends into the trouble, though. The truth is that I've always been someone who couldn't stand by when someone needed help. My magic first manifested when I confronted a few bullies. I didn't even know I was a witch before that, and learning I had magic simply meant I had a new tool to help people."

I suppose I shouldn't tell her the article she didn't like mentioned that. It'll only remind her that she's the Necessary Witch.

"You probably already know this," Alison began, "since everyone seems to know if only because they watched one of the movies made about the stupid adoption hearing, but I knew I was different because of my soul sight. I didn't know I was half-Drow for most of my childhood, so the idea of actually doing active magic was as new to me when I went to the School of Necessary Magic as it was for you. I had all kinds of difficulty with my magic at first, and I was very unsure of myself."

"The magic was overwhelming, but I was actually less intimidated than some of my friends," the agent admitted. "I was mostly in love with the school, especially the library."

"That's so cool," Hana declared and swayed slightly, her words slurred. "You're like sisters from another mother."

Raine looked thoughtful for a moment. "All the things that happened during Alison's time at the school made it safer overall for us. The wards and defenses were considerably stronger after all the stuff that transpired near the end of your time there."

Alison considered the explanation. The dark wizards and their actions at the School of Necessary Magic had shaped her entire adult life. Even when she attended a mundane college, she still spent time hunting dark wizards when she could, and they had haunted her thoughts until the final defeat of the Seventh Order.

Is that why I'm so obsessed with the Tapestry? Do I need a big villain to feed the insatiable appetite my previous obsession created?

She bit her lip. The implications tightened her stomach.

The FBI agent tilted her head and stared at Alison's hand.

"What's wrong?" she asked and glanced at her left hand. There were no marks or stray specks of wasabi.

The woman held her own left hand up and tapped an engagement ring. "We're alike in another way. I'm getting married in a few months myself. When's your wedding?"

Alison laughed, grateful to be pulled out of her dark thoughts, and looked at Mason. He shrugged, a silly grin on his face.

"We're still deciding," she explained. "I think we've put more thought into the honeymoon than we have the wedding. I'll let you in on a little secret. We're half-thinking about eloping."

"You should do it," Hana insisted. "It'll be fun."

"We'll have a very simple honeymoon, but we couldn't elope without annoying my fiancé's pack," Raine replied.

"Pack?" Alison asked. "He's a shifter?"

Raine nodded. "We're both busy with all kinds of things, so we want to get the ceremony done, but what about you? If you're so interested in a memorable honeymoon, I'm sure you have some great ideas about where to go."

Hana blew a raspberry. "Don't let them con you. Alison taking any real time off would be a miracle. She'll talk a good game and probably be back to work in two days with a big speech about how, 'Seattle needs me. The Mountain Strider might awaken at any moment.'"

"That's not true," Alison insisted. "We'll have a decent honeymoon. I'm even warming to the idea of an Oriceran honeymoon. Mason wants me to unplug."

Mason bobbed his head. "I do. Because Hana's right. If anyone can get hold of you, A, you'll spend the entire honeymoon calling Ava and asking if there's trouble."

The fox chuckled. "He so has your number." She filled her sake cup again and drained half of it with a slurp. "Going back to the ancestral homeland, Alison? Is that the idea?"

Raine watched with a curious look and soft smile.

Alison shook her head. "I am already getting too involved in this Drow stuff between Miar and Rasila. The last thing I need to do is put in a personal appearance in Drow territory. Nope, we'll be far away from them. I don't want anyone thinking I've come to Oriceran to make trouble."

The agent cleared her throat. "I might be able to help with that. I have a friend I went to school with, Christie. She works with a company that specializes in Earth to Oriceran tourism."

Alison frowned in thought. "Christie? As in Christie Bealls?"

"Yes. That's her."

"I knew her. So that's what she ended up doing?" She smiled. "Good for her. Somehow, that kind of fits, although I wondered if she'd end up a singer."

"She can probably help you find some good places to try. I know you don't have problems being around magic like many of the people she deals with, so it'll be even easier. I'll give you her number. No pressure. I'm merely trying to offer a resource."

"Thanks," Alison replied. She glanced at Mason. "If it's okay with you? I don't want you to think I'm railroading you."

"You're my boss, technically, and your dad's basically an overprotective living WMD. I'm already over the whole 'who's in charge' thing." He shrugged. "I don't think it would hurt to talk to her, but no guarantees, even if she is an old school friend of you both. It's kind of creepy. It's like the School of Necessary Magic alumni secretly control the world." He punctuated his sentence with a grin.

The women laughed.

Hana topped her cup off. "You know what we didn't do?" She waited until everyone looked at her. "We didn't toast to Blackthorn's arrest. That should have been the first thing we did."

Raine picked up her cup of tea. "That's definitely something to toast to. It's kind of weird. I've not let it sink in all the way, even though I've chased him from the start of my career." She lifted the cup higher. "To the arrest of Mr. Blackthorn."

Everyone else raised their cups. "To the arrest of Mr. Blackthorn," they chanted in unison.

The agent set her cup back on the table. "I have to admit I still can't get over you, Alison."

She took a sip of her drink before replying. "What do you mean? What about me?"

"You're so…normal." The woman looked down for a moment and concentration lined her face. "I always had this idea of you built up in my mind, both from things I heard when I was at school and later. It's not exactly like we're never briefed at the FBI on your activities, and that's not even counting situations like Carlyle where the agency ended up being involved in the end."

"So what did you think?" she asked.

"Only that you were different."

"You thought I was the raging and egomaniacal Dark Princess of Seattle?" Alison gobbled a quick bite of uni.

"Honestly, yes." Raine offered an apologetic smile.

Hana giggled. She was almost as red as a cooked lobster. "Don't let her fool you, Raine. Alison's worse than a princess. She's the Queen of Seattle, but she's a benevolent queen until you get her mad, and then she goes all 'Off with their heads!'"

Mason put his arm around Alison's shoulders. "We play things a little looser at our company than maybe you do at the FBI, Raine, but in the end, Alison always wants to help protect people. She gives everyone the opportunity to back down—more than most other people would. Unfortunately, many criminals are stubborn."

Raine waved her hands in front of her, a slightly panicked look on her face. "I know that. I experienced it firsthand with Blackthorn so I'm not accusing her of anything. It's only that she's a Drow princess and the adopted daughter of the Scourge of Harriken, and instead of planning which ancient Oriceran monster she'll confront next, she's getting married and worrying about her honeymoon. She's the kind of woman who has victory sushi after a job well done." A smile ate the panic. "That's what I'm getting at. Alison's merely a normal woman who happens to have unusually strong magic."

Alison beamed a smile at Mason and nodded at Raine. "That's a good description. I'm very much like you, Raine, and not only because we both got into trouble at school. I also can't stand bullies, and there are too many people and organizations in this world who like to bully others and think that magic or tech gives them that right. I'm here to tell them that no, they don't, especially in this city."

"You're right," the woman murmured. "We really are a lot alike. I wish I could have gone to school with you."

You say that, but then you would have been caught up with all the dark wizards. Not that you didn't have your own share of adventures.

Mason squeezed her shoulder and shook his head. "I don't know if that school could have taken two trouble-makers like you together, let alone adding Izzie into the mix. There would be nothing left there but a crater."

"Oh, that's right." Raine stared at her with something approaching almost awe for a moment. "The Fixer's daughter."

"I don't know what you have in your head, Raine, but Izzie's like me. She's simply a normal woman who happens to have considerable power."

"Izzie's cool," Hana agreed. "Maybe cooler than Alison. She has a more mysterious vibe around her."

"Thanks," Alison interjected.

"Just saying." The fox shrugged. "I love you, but you're not cool. Izzie? She's cool."

She chuckled. Her memories of the school were tied closely to the machinations of the dark wizards and their ultimate influence on her future and Izzie's, but she also had many good times with her friends during those four years. She only needed to allow herself to remember them. Having Raine there helped.

"I have a few questions," Raine stated. "I wondered if you can tell me about Dorvu and how that all happened. Everyone was so matter-of-fact about a dragon being there."

Alison smiled softly. "I would love to tell you. The thing you have to understand was that, at first, he was nothing but an egg."

CHAPTER SIXTEEN

The afternoon sun reflected off the tranquil water and Alison smiled as she settled on her couch, a glass of orange juice on a coaster on the coffee table in front of her. The almost perfect vista never failed to soothe her. The view from her condo had been great, but there was something about sitting in her own home that eased her perpetually anxious soul.

I really should decide what to do with that condo. Wait. What I am doing? I am finally letting things be slow, and I instantly try to fill my head with more stuff to stress over.

She chuckled and shook her head. Perhaps she should sit on the edge of her jetty and simply watch the water, or even take up fishing. It'd be an interesting way to fill her time off.

Despite Hana's accusations, she had taken a few days off. She deserved it after helping the FBI capture a dangerous criminal, but she still had a hard time shutting her mind off or resisting the urge to call around asking about trouble in Seattle.

Her friend was half-right. There was no way she would be able to clock out for any significant length of time and enjoy her honeymoon with her current state of mind and habit of worrying. She needed to work her way to being able to take an extended time out—perhaps even a month—for her honeymoon. Stepping away from the day-to-day running of the company now and again in the lead-up to the wedding would be a good way to accomplish that goal.

I have a few minutes. I might as well check in.

Alison gave in to the impulse and pulled her phone out. She dialed Shay.

"Hey, Alison," her mother answered. "I meant to call you about helping the FBI. Your dad joked about Brownstone arresting gnome masterminds being a new family tradition. Now, I feel like I need to find some gnome super-criminal and stop him, too."

"Oh, yeah, that. I didn't call about that and the FBI did most of the hard work. I only blew some guys up."

"That's basically what it means to be a Brownstone. You blow things up and eat delicious food afterwards." Shay chuckled. "If you're not calling to brag, what are you calling about? Not that I mind, of course."

"I simply wanted to check in. I'll have a sibling in only a few months, after all." She exhaled a happy sigh. "It's hard for me to believe at times, and I can only imagine what you're going through as the clock ticks down. You always seem okay when I call, but I wanted to be sure."

Shay scoffed. "That's the thing. I'm not going through anything. Sure, I'm not as mobile I used to be, but that's a temporary problem. The earlier months weren't always fun, but I didn't have as much morning sickness as some people I know. The cravings were annoying, but I haven't really had to deal with those in a while."

Alison leaned back on the couch and crossed her legs. "I know you've never been one to whine about being pregnant, Mom, but you are still in the middle of something that's a big deal, and it's the one thing you can't get through by simply doing more research or finding a bigger gun."

"The only thing I've worried about is your dad, and once he got his self-pity out of his system during his last road trip, he's been fine." The woman snickered. "We did need to have a little discussion the other day about how the kid won't grill their own meat when they're two. Apparently, James thought that was a perfectly reasonable idea. Sometimes, I honestly don't know what goes through his head."

"That does sound like Dad." Alison took a deep breath. "Are you still set on not finding out the sex? It's not too late. The baby is due in July, right? It hasn't suddenly started super-growing or anything weird."

"Yes," Shay replied. "If anything, it's shocking how normal everything's turned out. The baby is normal size, growing at the normal rate, and exhibits all the normal and expected things. I'm not saying I thought there would be a tail or anything, but you're right, it's been hard to be sure."

Alison didn't even want to begin to try to understand how the development of a partially alien baby with mostly human DNA might proceed. There was probably no one on Earth who could truly predict that.

Or is there?

She frowned and thought back to Ava's discussion with her concerning the CIA's Non-Oriceran Alien Taskforce.

Were they poring over Shay's medical records, looking for clues?

It can't be that obvious. After all, Dad's test results were normal enough for most of his life that no one could identify him as alien. Whispy did a good job of modifying him, so shouldn't it follow that his biological child will be as human as me?

Alison grinned. Not as human as her. She was only half-human, and there were many people in Seattle who reminded her of that.

"Alison," Shay prodded over the line. "Are you there?"

"Sorry, Mom. I was a little distracted, but don't think I didn't notice how you dodged my question."

"How did I dodge your question?"

"You didn't tell me if you were interested in finding out the sex of the baby," she reminded her.

"Oh, that? Nope. We don't care. I wondered if I would care eventually, but the more I have thought about it, the less I find I care. I think James would prefer a son since he already has you, but we've all seen that it doesn't matter if he has a boy or a girl. He'll treat them the same. But why are you asking about this now?"

"I don't know," she mused. "It's something that's going through my mind. Meeting someone who went to my school has got me thinking about both the past and the future. I'm not having kids anytime soon, but I'm thinking more about the baby, anyway."

"Do you have regrets?" Shay asked, the humor gone from her voice. If anyone understood running from their past, it was her.

"Not as many as you might think. There are things I wish had happened differently, but I also know that most of those weren't my fault, especially the dark wizards messing with me at school." She shifted forward on the couch, her brow furrowed. "I've also thought about my company lately. I always seem to be undecided about whether I should expand it. I have a good primary team of magicals, and Jerry's team is great. We recently had a few new non-magical hires, but every time I think about bringing on someone new to my primary team, I find some reason why it's a bad idea. Now, I question that."

Her mother chuckled. "Maybe you should listen to yourself then, Alison."

"But I might not make the right decision. I'm half-convinced it's because I'm worried about other people getting hurt and things like that, but even Dad needs help on occasion." She sighed.

"Trust your instincts," Shay replied. "If it was about you trying to do everything yourself, you wouldn't ever bring any of the others along. Shit, you brought your fiancé to help you apprehend Blackthorn, but that's a good thing, too."

"Because I had backup?" Alison asked.

"I thought more along the lines of 'couples who share common interests will have stronger marriages,'" Shay clarified.

Alison laughed. "I didn't think of it that way. I've wondered, at times, whether it's a good thing to work with the man I love, but you and Dad used to go on tomb raids together far more than you do now."

"Yeah, it's not a big deal. It'd be more of a problem if he was a pencil pusher or something and couldn't relate to me. But he's a tough guy in his own right and most importantly, he loves me. That's the big thing in the end." Shay chuckled. "Ah, I'm getting too sentimental now that I'm pregnant, but that doesn't make it any less true. I'm glad to see you found someone, and I think you two go well together. I think Mason's a good guy, and he has enough of a backbone to stand up to you—and, for that matter, to stand up to your father, which means he has balls of steel."

She grinned. "That's true. I was worried I'd never be able to get Dad's approval for any man. The only reason Tanner and I worked out was because Dad was thousands of miles away most of the time." She took deep breath and her stomach tightened. "There's something else I wanted to bounce off you about the wedding. I know it's my wedding, but it's also a family thing and you should have input."

Shay grunted. "Don't start thinking that way. What I want and what your Dad want aren't important. It's your wedding, so you should go about it however you want."

"I was kind of..." Alison sighed. "I don't know. I thought about some quickie thing. A couple of witnesses and a big honeymoon for, like, a month. I've considered that more and more lately. The idea of a big wedding—let alone like the one you and Dad had—kind of wigs me out."

"Then don't have a big wedding," her mother replied, her voice gentle. "If you simply want to have a couple of your friends as witnesses and use the courthouse and a Justice of the Peace, do it. In the end, you're up there, and your husband isn't someone we knew before he met you. You don't owe us a big ceremony."

"But Dad will be pissed," she replied. "Won't he?"

"I doubt it. Other than barbecue and Father McCartney, it's not like he had many specific requirements for our wedding. The only reason the proposal became a big thing is because I made it that way."

Thomas barked over the line.

"Quiet, dog," Shay commanded. "I'm on the phone here. No. Don't look at me like that. If you want to go beg for steak, wait until James comes home." She cleared her throat. "Sorry about that, Alison. You know Thomas. He's getting crankier as he gets older, except with James, but I think that's merely James being the ultimate alpha. No animal will fuck with him."

"Do you really think Dad wouldn't be angry about the wedding?" she asked. "I don't want to start our marriage with Dad's disapproval."

"Your dad will be fine," she replied and punctuated it with a little growl. "And if he's not, I'll make sure he is."

"I'm not trying to cause trouble, Mom."

"It isn't about that. You need to live for yourself, Alison, not for us. You have a great start already, and this continues that. I have my career, and he has his restaurant. We both have a new child coming who will keep us busy. We love you and we always want to be there for you, but as parents, our greatest hope is for you to continue living as a proud and independent woman. That means sometimes, you'll need to tell us to back the hell off or to mind our own business. You're a Brownstone, which means you don't let anyone tell you what to do, even other Brownstones."

Alison smiled. "Okay, Mom, I'll keep that in mind, but you might want to lay a few hints out for Dad to soften the blow if I do decide to skip a big ceremony."

"I've been married to him for a while now. I know how

to manage him. Don't worry." Shay yawned. "Oof. I'm sorry, Alison. I've been tired a lot lately and am sleeping for two now. Do you mind if I cut this call short?"

"No, go ahead," she replied warmly. "I'll talk to you soon, Mom. I love you."

"I love you, too. Again, good job on that Blackthorn thing."

"Thanks."

Shay ended the call.

Alison tossed her phone on the couch cushion and her thoughts swirled with possibilities. The appeal of a special honeymoon and a quick wedding grew with each passing day, and with both Mason and Shay now onboard, little guilt remained.

A frown crept onto her face. "I swear if Drow princesses show up to mess with my wedding, I'll kill them all."

CHAPTER SEVENTEEN

The Overseer stood in the center of the unfurnished circular white room and surveyed the suited and almost identical men who stood against the walls. The Weavers were his hands, as he was the hands of the Source. Their actions would determine the future of the Tapestry and Earth. They had laid so many plans with such care but now, everything was in jeopardy.

All their meticulous calculations had been found wanting, if not entirely useless. Alison Brownstone was a disruptive variable. The surprising incompetence of earlier Strands had led to the escape of the target now guarded by her and her people. For the first time since their arrival on Earth, simple recalculation didn't seem to bring the most likely results. Adjustments in strategy were necessary—perhaps even some that humans would consider desperate.

"The plan must succeed," the Overseer intoned as he looked at the blank-faced Weavers. "The failure of the Ultimate project has robbed us of new, more powerful Strands and wasted significant resources. The time for the plan grows short, and we have not created a sufficient number of Strands for our ultimate goal. The window of Earth's interface with the Source grows smaller with each passing day. Analysis indicates a less than 0.0004 percent probability of success if we wait more than six weeks. It shrinks to one tenth of that if we wait twelve weeks."

The Weavers watched him and blinked occasionally but did little else. There was no hint of fear or discomfort on their faces. They listened patiently, being granted context while they awaited orders.

Failure would mean the death of all the Tapestry, but the thought didn't trouble the Overseer, nor did it trouble the Weavers. Fear was for the primitive natural animals populating Earth and Oriceran and unnecessary for the tools of the Source. The Overseer was created without such unnecessary mental inconveniences, and he had created the Weavers in the same way. All they needed to do to succeed was execute their orders based on the most likely probabilities calculated after careful consideration of all relevant variables.

That would bring the victory. It had to. They had no other choice on how to behave. No options were available. Even the Overseer was limited. The Source had crafted him that way.

A Weaver tilted his head to the side. "The depletion of Strand forces has made any large-scale activities implausible, let alone an attempt to retake the target. Alison Brownstone and her allies always keep the creature close to them. All calculations suggest they will repel our forces at our current strength."

"That is all true," the Overseer replied, his voice as flat

and lifeless as the Weaver's. "Therefore, we must increase the strength and number of our forces. Accordingly, the collection of alternative raw materials must be accelerated. We must achieve rapid growth of our offensive potential."

"There is a difficulty," another Weaver offered. "Did not the last general analysis suggest a 99.4 percent probability that human authorities will recognize the abnormal collection pattern and interfere? At least some Strands have been sighted and per orders, we have minimized the killing of human witnesses."

"The human authorities are irrelevant," the Overseer declared, and his hands hung limply at his sides. "They are slow to act and display disunity. We will have completed our task before they can respond effectively."

"But there is a high probability the humans will assume a necromancer is responsible," the Weaver replied. "If so, it's unlikely that only local authorities would be involved. We risk greater exposure. Our forces are insufficient to withstand the entirety of the human resources available in this city, even with the recent modifications of the Strands."

The Overseer stared at him. There was no irritation. He was merely performing his function.

"Our last analysis also indicated only a 39.3 percent probability that Alison Brownstone will take notice or involve herself in our collection process," he replied. "Further calculation also makes it clear that without sufficient Strands, we will be unable to achieve all necessary remaining goals. If we do not pursue additional resources, the plan will fail. We will be destroyed, and the Source will be unable to come.

"All are irrelevant with the exception of Alison Brownstone. She is the only variable that has resulted in continued disruption to our efforts. The deaths of any others are irrelevant. By the time the humans understand what is happening, it won't matter. The Source will be here, and the humans will have little ability to stop it. The Source will rise up and Earth will become the Source. Once Earth is secured, the Source will take Oriceran. We must accelerate collection. The Strands must be replenished. All other considerations are secondary, including individual Strand survival."

The Weavers nodded.

One stepped forward. "And if Alison Brownstone does get involved?"

"We will continue to execute the previously established backup procedures," the Overseer explained. "The short-term sacrifice of Strands will allow us time for greater build-up. Once we have sufficient resources, we will recover the target and finish the plan. There is a greater chance of success than failure, so there is therefore no reason not to pursue the plan given the consequences of failing."

A tiny distracting sliver of something pricked the Overseer's mind. He wasn't sure what it was at first. All the probabilities and plans were there, but he lingered excessively on the possibility of failure. The sensation was unsettling.

Is this fear? How utterly useless. We need the Source before we become too human.

CHAPTER EIGHTEEN

*H**uh. This is about the last thing I would have ever thought
I needed to add to this place when I started this company.*

Alison knelt to press her hand against the artificial
grass that filled the large room. Ava tapped her ever-
present tablet behind her. Cardboard tubes and perches
filled the room, along with smaller fenced areas and even a
few terrariums on stands lining the walls. It was the
Brownstone Security indoor pet park, but there was only
one animal in it. Omni, in small brown cat form, lay on a
cushion in the center of the room. He raised his head to
meow once at the two women before he snuggled into the
cushion again, a bored look on his face.

"I don't get it." She stood. "Everyone seemed really
enthusiastic about this place when I announced it, but no
one's brought their pets except Hana."

Her assistant looked up from her tablet. "Jerry brings
his dog sometimes, Miss Brownstone." She pushed her
glasses up her nose and looked at Alison, a curious glint in
her eyes. "Do you regret building it?"

She sighed. "Not really. It is a nice perk, especially if Tahir gets the pooper-scooper drone working like he said. Besides, if it does nothing but help us keep an eye on Omni, it'll be worth it."

Ava looked over her shoulder to verify that they were alone. "Do you think the Tapestry has given up?"

"A few weeks ago I might have said no, but I'm not so sure anymore." She shrugged. "They're obviously still around. They supplied Tatum the cores but now, no one can find their scent. They've lost men and they've lost considerable resources. They might be bleeding out as an organization, especially if they are simply some weird magical cult."

"Perhaps whatever they needed Omni for is simply not worth the cost," the other woman suggested. "In all matters, the cost versus benefit ratio must be considered, cult or...otherwise."

"You still think they're aliens, don't you?" Alison tried to not let the doubt creep into her voice.

"The thought has crossed my mind more than a few times, yes."

"Who knows? All I know is I want to finish them." She walked over to the cat and knelt to stroke his fur. "What are you really, Omni? The ultimate alien pet?"

He meowed in response.

She pushed to her feet. "At least all the cameras we have in here keep him from changing, even if people constantly ask about why Hana has so many pets. I simply—" Her phone rang. She pulled it out and chuckled after looking at the caller ID. "So much for taking it easy."

Ava's lips pressed into a thin line, and her forehead crinkled. "Who is it?"

"Agent Latherby." She brought the phone to her ear and accepted the call. "What's up?"

"I have an important if unusual matter I wish to discuss with you, Miss Brownstone," the agent replied. "I'd like to meet with you today if at all possible."

"One sec." She lowered her phone and looked at Ava. "How's my schedule for today?"

"Quite open," the other woman clarified. "Per your instructions."

She brought the phone back to her ear. "When did you want to meet?"

Agent Latherby sat in his chair, his fingers laced together on his desk in front of his keyboard. He wore a deep frown on his face. He glanced at the computer screen before he looked at Alison again.

He looks more upset than usual, but if it were an emergency, he wouldn't ask about meetings.

She settled into her seat. "What's the deal, Latherby? Even Helen was bitchier than usual, but I've not heard anything from my informants since the Blackthorn affair. He didn't escape, did he?"

If he did, Raine will be seriously pissed.

"Blackthorn? No, he's very secure. This has nothing to do with Blackthorn to the best of my knowledge, but strange connections often manifest in my line of work." He unlaced his fingers, but his frown remained. "I suppose that's part of my frustration. I find myself annoyed because no matter how many irritations and unusual events that occur in this job, I often find myself still surprised by what actually happens. It makes it hard to get in front of trouble before it comes."

Alison nodded. "I can understand that. So what does this have to do with me? Did the government lose another secret project who is now terrorizing tourists or something?"

Agent Latherby snorted. "If only it were so straight-forward. Before I explain why I called you, I need to first provide some background."

"Go ahead."

"It's recently come to the attention of the police that bodies have disappeared around town. The nature of the disappearances suggests that magicals might be involved, so they've asked for FBI and PDA aid in investigating."

She frowned, totally surprised by the information. "Bodies are missing? You mean like dead bodies?"

Ugh. I don't like where this is going.

He nodded. "Yes, dead bodies. Corpses, if you will. Initially, they were taken mostly from funeral homes, but now some of the...fresher bodies from cemeteries have also disappeared. At first, the police assumed this was some kind of organ-snatching ring. It's not impossible, of course. Some illegal transplant operations use magic to bridge the gap given how total healing of a cirrhotic liver, for example, is far more difficult than using magic to lower the chance of rejection."

Alison's frown deepened to a scowl. "But since when

does the PDA care about the illegal organ trade? Isn't that more an FBI matter?"

"You're right, but taking bodies from the graveyard—even relatively fresh bodies—severely undermines that as a possibility. We have to assume there is something else at play." Agent Latherby's expression settled into grim lines.

She groaned. "A necromancer? I hate zombies."

"Does anyone like them? I doubt even the necromancers care for them all that much." He shook his head. "But we doubt it's a necromancer. If it were as simple as that, the AET or PDA could handle it, or we could identify the magical and set the bounty hunters onto them."

"But if you're involved and not merely the local cops, it means magicals, right? What other kind of magical would care so much about dead bodies?"

The agent nodded. "The obvious was tried. We attempted to track the bodies with different types of spells, including direct tracking, scrying, and other variants. They all failed."

"That makes sense," she replied. "There's no point in stealing bodies if all it takes is one wizard to track you and set AET on you."

"True enough." His mouth curled downward into a grimace. "But that is where things become questionable."

"Questionable? What do you mean?"

"Because the tracking issue goes beyond that," Agent Latherby explained. "It's not as if the cemeteries and funeral homes lack cameras. In every case where there was an active camera in the line of sight, the video is conveniently disrupted."

Alison's stomach tightened.

It couldn't be. Could it?

"Maybe they have the services of a good infomancer or they learned the necessary spells to cover their tracks," she suggested. Her heart pounded.

He nodded. "That's true enough, so I tested a theory. I went so far as to contact friends of mine at a few different agencies. There are many satellites in orbit at any given time, and at least some of them have line-of-sight on Seattle at every minute of the day." He turned his monitor to face her.

She squinted and tilted her head, not sure what she was looking at. After a moment, she realized it was an overhead picture of a neighborhood—Eastlake, from the look of it, given the presence of Lake Union to the west and Gas Works Park across the water. She'd flown over it enough times to recognize it, even if she had stuck to a modest altitude. There was a small multi-colored blotch in the southeast of the image.

Alison stared at the screen and tried to discern the identity of the blob. "What am I looking at other than Seattle?"

"A representative satellite image," Agent Latherby explained.

She pointed at the discoloration. "And this is what exactly?"

"That's a good question." He nodded toward the screen. "I could show you other images taken over several minutes and all similar. The shadow moves." He pointed at it. "But do you recognize where this is?"

Her eyes narrowed, she leaned forward and focused before she sucked in a breath. "It's the cemetery. I assume the appearance of that is coordinated timewise with weird camera activity?" She sighed.

"You've reached the same conclusion I have, I presume." Agent Latherby turned his screen back toward him.

"Those Tapestry bastards have demonstrated weird anti-tracking capabilities," she muttered. "It's not like they're the only people who can pull it off, but it's not been all that long after all the Ultimate crap involving Tapestry True Cores, so it'd make sense to think it's them."

"Exactly." The PDA agent entered a few commands into his computer. "Based on some of the things you've told us and the timing, as you just highlighted, it would be irresponsible to dismiss their possible involvement. Given that you've dealt with them before and seem to be a particular focus of theirs, I thought it best to make you aware of this. The only thing that doesn't fit is the nature of the crime. From what you told me before, they didn't demonstrate necromancy."

Alison looked to the side and shook her head slightly. "That's true. I assume that at least someone among them has life magic potential because of how they look so similar. They didn't cast regular spells themselves, but after what I saw with Ultimate, it might be because they've modified themselves in similar ways as those I saw. But every time we've faced them, they seemed to be alive."

"But you inflicted considerable losses on them in your previous encounters. Also, if they were behind Ultimate, it means you've cut off additional resources," he observed.

"Do you think they're turning to zombies because they're desperate?" Alison grimaced. "At least they'll be slow."

Agent Latherby ran a hand over his scalp, a deep frown on his face. "There's still so much we don't know about the Tapestry, but I've been in this job too long to ignore it when the evidence points to something obvious. Unfortunately, no one has been able to catch them in the process, even with people being more alert in recent days."

"I haven't even heard about this," she pointed out. "Is it really that widespread?"

"Extremely so. The Seattle PD has kept quiet about this while all the various law enforcement agencies look into it. We've managed to convince the media to keep their mouths shut for at least a few more days, but that won't last. Some of the local funeral homes admitted to losing bodies when questioned, but the police only became aware of it when a few morticians reached out to them, worried about necromancers. It won't be long before this leaks out or the media goes ahead with the story. We would all prefer that the issue be resolved before then. The last thing we need is this city panicking about zombie hordes."

The agent scoffed. "Too many movies have filled people's heads with stupid ideas. I'm not saying necromancy isn't disgusting, but we'd see people locking themselves in and stockpiling weapons, convinced they could be turned into a zombie by a bite or a scratch. After decades of open magic, the average person still doesn't have a clue how it works."

Alison sighed and nodded. "And you want me to track the Tapestry and end the threat?"

"That would be optimal, but we both know it's not that easy for the very reasons we believe they're involved. In this case, it's not so much that I'm asking you to find and eliminate the Tapestry. Their possible involvement with Ultimate is more than enough to get all the relevant local and federal investigators we've needed to look into them, and we're following up various leads." Agent Latherby shook his head. "No, this is merely a courtesy—a warning. We don't have the personnel to watch you constantly, and I don't think you would want or appreciate it. But everything you've told us suggests the Tapestry will target you, your people, and that creature. Whatever move they intend to make, it'll be soon. When they do, you need to pass any information along, as whatever scheme they have obviously extends beyond stealing your employee's pet."

"Fair enough," she replied. "And if I happen to wipe them all out before the PDA can get to them?"

He shrugged. "I have far too many cases and not enough resources to work them. I won't be upset if you don't add to that workload."

CHAPTER NINETEEN

This is a plan, Alison thought. *Not necessarily a good plan, but it's a plan. And we're finally doing something proactive. Kind of.*

Hana shivered and tightened her hand around the Omni's long leash. He was currently in the form of a small brown dog. She walked him up the sidewalk along a tall gray fence with Drysi, Mason, and Alison behind them. Even at night, the bright lights of the city washed out many of the stars, but the cloudless sky revealed a few pinpricks in the firmament. The noise of cars lay distant, and few animals moved amongst the darkened gravestones and tombs behind the fence.

The fox pointed at a flickering lamp post. "Did we really have to do this at night?"

Alison shrugged. "There's more chance the Tapestry will show up when there are less people around. They might be ruthless freaks, but they like to hide. They know we can kick their asses, and I'm sure they aren't railgun proof, either."

Drysi snickered. "Since when are you afraid of the bloody Tapestry, Hana?"

Hana sniffed. She gestured widely with her free hand. "I'm not worried about the Tapestry or zombies, but I don't like being around graveyards. It's hard to know where the veil is thin, and I don't want to end up in the World in Between. A lot of places like this were selected in the past because the veil was thin to begin with, and it's only worse now with all the magic flowing back to Earth."

Alison shook her head. "But this location isn't that old. It wasn't built over an existing burial mound or anything. This isn't some ancient spirit site. It's only a graveyard."

"Only a graveyard," the woman mumbled. "I keep thinking about the kemana ruins. Sometimes, I wonder if the veil between worlds around all of Seattle is thin."

"I think we would know if that was a problem," Mason suggested with a shrug. "It's not like people go missing from Seattle cemeteries all the time. The PDA would spend more time spirit-whacking if they needed to."

"No, people don't disappear, only bodies." Hana rolled her eyes. "It's totally safe here," she added in a mocking deep voice.

"That's all recent," her boss insisted. "Sonya, do you see anything with your drones?"

While the girl worked close support for the team, Tahir concentrated, off-comms, on running a dozen magic- and algorithm-supported drones throughout the city to watch other cemeteries for anything suspicious.

"Nah," Sonya replied through the ear receiver. "I've checked with different spectra, but no one looks freaky or weird. There are a few people walking nearby—about fifty yards away—but I can see them. There's nothing weird happening to my feed, and they don't look like the Strands. No suits."

"They might sneak into the areas using invisibility," Mason suggested.

Hana frowned. "Spirits can be invisible, too." She glanced at Omni. The dog padded along and wagged his tail without any hint of tension. "I also don't like the idea of risking Omni out in the open like this at night. We have no guarantee my little baby will throw a tantrum even if the Tapestry shows up."

Tantrum? Is that what we call the battle form?

"I'm sorry," Alison responded. "The PDA and everyone else might be looking for the Tapestry, but we're the only ones with decent bait and I'd rather we set the trap on our own terms. If we try to ask the government, they'll probably reconsider taking him, and I think we would all rather that not happen. The last thing I want is a confrontation with the feds."

Hana glowered. "They'd better stay away from him." She sighed at her pet. "Don't worry, baby. Mommy will keep the mean government agents away from you."

Or he'll tear them to pieces. Damn. We do need to handle this ourselves.

Alison stared at Omni. He was at the source of everything, but she still wasn't totally sure why the Tapestry wanted him. Then again, she also hadn't been sure what the Seventh Order wanted Izzie for until close to the end. Sometimes, it wasn't necessary to know why her enemies did what they did to stop them.

"We might get lucky," she suggested. "He might be able to sense them coming."

She wasn't convinced of that given that Omni hadn't demonstrated the skill in previous encounters, but she was running out of ideas. The Tapestry's abilities helped them defy tracking, magical or technological. To the best of her knowledge, now that Alphonse Tatum was dead, the group possessed no link to the underworld she could exploit or follow, regardless of what informant she pressured. When they were quiet and did nothing obvious, it was easy to ignore them, but the idea that they might be behind body-snatching made bile rise in the back of her throat. She couldn't wait around for them to make their next move.

"I like walking at night," Drysi admitted. "There's something calming about it. We live in such a busy world. It's a good feeling when it slows down. I probably would have been a much happier woman if I'd grown up in some tiny county village rather than Cardiff, I won't lie." She uttered a slow chuckle. "But you know, everyone from the PDA to you, Alison, seems convinced it's those bloody freaks. What if it's simply a normal necromancer having a good time?"

Mason grunted and uncharacteristic hatred flashed in his eyes. "There's nothing wrong with eliminating a necromancer. They're abominations."

"What he said," Alison agreed. "My gut tells me it's not merely a normal necromancer, but if it is, we'll deal with him." She laughed at a thought that flashed through her head.

Her friends all stared at her like she'd lost it.

She shrugged. "Think about how messed up our lives

are that I can say something like 'merely a normal necromancer' like it's no big deal."

Drysi smirked. "You're bloody right."

Hana slowed to allow Omni to sniff some flowers. "At least it's not a giant necromancer. Imagine if the Mountain Strider could summon skeletons or zombies to fight with it."

Alison tried not to laugh again at the mental image of a giant zombie Mountain Strider on the rampage through Seattle. It wasn't as if something like that was impossible, but even with magic now flowing into the world, certain practical realities constrained her likely foes. A megalomaniacal gnome was a reasonable expectation, a zombie giant not as much. Then again, she took a shape-changing mysterious creature past a cemetery to try to bait a group who, in the best-case scenario, might be a magical cult willing to change people's faces and bodies. Of course, in the worst-case scenario, they could be a group of non-Oriceran aliens planning something deadly.

Hana stopped and her gaze lingered on a gravestone on the other side of the fence. "Here lies Millicent Tavers. 1884 to 1903. Taken far too soon. May she find rest with the Lord." She narrowed her eyes.

"Hana?" her boss prompted.

The fox continued to stare at the grave and her mouth twitched. She uttered a quiet growl and Omni responded with one of his own.

"Hana?" Alison called again and she stiffened instinctively.

"Don't you see it?" the other woman murmured.

The dog stopped growling.

Mason slipped his hand under his jacket and grabbed his wand. "See what?"

Drysi moved her head from side to side, her hand resting on her holstered pistol. "The bastards are around here?"

Alison didn't sense any unusual magic, but maybe her friend smelled something. "Do you see Strands? Are you're sure they're not simply boring-looking guys in suits? Sonya?"

"I don't see anything," the girl replied, her voice pitched higher than normal.

Hana's head snapped toward Alison. She blinked a few times and laughed. "Oh, sorry. No, no. I don't see any Strands. There's no trouble." She tilted her head and looked up. "None that's coming right away."

Mason holstered his wand with a slight frown. Drysi responded with an amused snicker.

"Why were you so obsessed with that grave?" Alison asked.

Omni sat on his haunches and tilted his head as he watched Hana.

"I think graveyards spook me not because I worry about spirits but because they make me think about death in a way that I don't normally," the fox explained. "I know we deal with it in our work, but that's all in the moment. This..." She gestured toward the grave. "It isn't like that. This is the place you can't avoid even if you have an easy office job with no guns or artifacts. Even gnomes die, but it got me thinking, and I think I had some sort of lateral breakthrough."

Alison folded her arms, now more confused than concerned. "About what?"

"What if we're thinking about all this the wrong way?" Hana crouched to scratch Omni behind the ears. He leaned into it.

Mason and Drysi surveyed the darkness, both their faces lined with residual tension. Flipping the switch between being battle ready and not wasn't that easy.

"How are we thinking about this the wrong way?" Alison asked, her own heart still pounding a little harder than it should for a nighttime stroll, even one past a graveyard.

"We always assume that this is about necromancers or the Tapestry making zombies." Her forehead wrinkled. "But if the Tapestry could make zombies, we probably would have seen them before. We fought enough of them."

"Maybe, but they might be desperate. The Strands were impressive in their own ways, or maybe they don't have enough True Cores left to fuel their powers."

The fox shook her head. "The Strands all kind of look alike, right? They're all brown-haired white guys in the same suit. They aren't identical, but they're very similar."

"What are you getting at?"

Hana patted Omni's head before she straightened. "You can all cast spells, so you're used to thinking about making something from nothing."

Alison shook her head. "It's not like that. There are limits. We still have to draw on magical power."

Drysi scoffed. "And not all of us are as powerful as the Dark Princess over there." She opened her jacket to reveal her vest filled with sheathed knives and patted the hilt of one. "And this is why I enchant all these nice little toys beforehand and still use a gun. It makes for a tidy fight, and it means I strain my magic less."

Mason nodded. "My family specializes in healing, but it's not like even the best healers can bring someone back from the dead. There are limits even to spells."

"Sure," Hana replied, and her brown eyes widened with apparent insight. "But the point is..." She dropped the leash. Her tails appeared, and her claws extended. Vulpine yellow eyes replaced the dark-brown human ones. "I can do many things with no strain, but they are very specific things."

Omni barked and ran around her in circles, wagging his tail.

"I get it." Alison's breath caught. "We've not seen the Tapestry show anything approaching general magic. I've assumed lately that they might have a couple of high-powered magicals modifying their followers, but what if they don't at all?"

Drysi's face pinched in confusion. "I don't follow either of you."

Mason nodded his agreement. "Me neither."

The fox pointed at the graveyard. "Raw materials, except not as zombies. But at least that way, they don't have to conjure anything."

"They shape them into the Strands?" Drysi asked.

"Maybe." A shudder surged through Hana.

Alison surveyed the graveyard slowly and searched for even a hint of a humanoid shape. "That would explain why the Strands look so similar and also why they act the way they do. They must imbue them with at least some will.

They aren't totally mindless corpses, but they don't seem all that independent either."

"So they are bloody zombies, then," Drysi declared with a shrug. "I don't get how it's different."

"Maybe more like flesh robots," Mason suggested, his disdain written on his face. "It's like Alison said. They aren't shambling and mindless. But that still means someone has to create them. There's a Dr. Frankenstein hiding out there and directing all this."

Alison fixed her gaze on Millicent Tavers' grave. Targeting Hana was a personal insult and more than enough to earn Alison's ire. Flooding the streets with Ultimate was a threat to the living but now, even the dead couldn't rest easy.

I need to find whoever is behind all this and end them.

"Agent Latherby is right," she murmured. "They're coming soon. That's why they're on the recruiting drive."

"Good," Drysi declared. "I'm tired of waiting for the bloody bastards, and it's nice to be able to cut loose now and again against garbage."

Hana smiled at Omni. "I only want my baby safe."

"They're death lords," Mason muttered through gritted teeth. "The sooner we end them, the better." He shook his head. "But we can't spend months walking past cemeteries and hoping we get lucky."

Alison tore her gaze away from the tombstone. "I have an idea, but it's one I don't think Tahir will like. Sonya, go ahead and get his attention and tell him to get on the comms."

CHAPTER TWENTY

Hana bounced a little where she sat on Alison's couch, a huge grin on her face. Omni, in ferret form, lay curled in a nearby chair, his eyes closed. Alison rested in a chair beside the couch. Mason remained upstairs taking a long shower.

He seemed a little tense. I never realized how much he hated necromancers. It makes sense, though—life versus death.

"It's like old times!" Hana declared and yanked Alison out of her thoughts. "The best friends living under the same roof again. It's destiny."

Sonya emerged from the kitchen, a cup of steaming hot chocolate in hand. She rolled her eyes. "It's not a slumber party, Hana. This is a mission." She raised her cup and adopted a serious look, which came off somewhat ridiculous given her youth and her ratty hoody. "The Tapestry is on the move, and we have to be ready." She punctuated her sentence with a sip.

Hana scoffed. "How can you be so young yet already so boring?"

"I'm not boring. I'm focused."

Alison sighed. "She's right, you know, Hana. I don't know if this will work, but it's worth a shot, and if does, it'll get messy."

I guess it's a good thing I didn't buy a boat yet. The Tapestry would simply sink it when they attack.

"I'm not complaining," Hana replied. "But I don't see how me staying here makes it any more likely that the Tapestry will try to take Omni." She stretched out, laid on her side on the couch, and rested her head in the palm of her hand, her elbow down. "If they really wanted to take him, why not do it at my place? I'm tough, but I don't keep the *tachi* there, even if I do have the ring, and Tahir's better behind a computer than he is at throwing fireballs."

"Your apartment is also in the middle of the city," Alison replied. "They might have their weird stealth magic, but they're not invisible. If an army of suited freaks arrives and attacks a building, people will call the cops, and the AET will rain power-armored agents on them in minutes." She pointed to a window. "We're not totally isolated here, but if a mysterious group showed up and attacked us, there would be a delay before reinforcements arrived, even with dropships. Given the attitude of some of the people around here, they might not even call the police because they know this is my house, and they might simply decide it's my problem to resolve." She frowned. "Besides, if the Tapestry intend to make a move, I'd prefer there be fewer other people around. Sonya can do her thing hidden easily enough, and all we have to do is throw Omni in a closet, wait for him to come out as Angry Omni, and we're good to go. That means we have almost a full team under one roof. I wouldn't have minded if Tahir wanted to stay, and Drysi—"

"I know, I know. She laughed at the idea to your face. I was there." Hana chuckled. "As for my handsome, intelligent but stubborn boyfriend..." She rolled her eyes. "I asked him again about it when we were alone, and he whined about having to stay somewhere he wasn't comfortable. What a big baby."

Alison puffed her cheeks and blew a breath out. "I can understand. You're his girlfriend, and I might be his friend, but I'm also his boss. I thought about doing this at Brownstone Security, but we have no idea how long this will take, and it's not exactly a hotel."

Sonya dropped on the edge of a chair and sipped her hot chocolate with a frustrated look. "It'd get annoying if we were together all day and all night. He'd probably order me around. He's a great mentor, but he can be too much at times."

Hana grinned. "He can be bossy. He tries with me but no one can tame this Hot Fox." Her grin faded, and something approaching an actual serious expression made it onto her face. "He might end up coming here if this goes on long enough."

"I don't want this to go on too long," Alison explained. "The PDA and the Seattle PD are looking into this, but I'm trying to push this along as much as possible. I'll reach out to Vincent and all my other contacts. This is one time where some of my other street contacts can do something for me that will help them out and not require them to do much other than spend some time keeping an eye on cemeteries. It's an easy job for the ex-gang members. I'll make it clear they'll risk dying if they try to fight the Tapestry if they see them. All they have to do is call me in. I'd have them call the cops, but most of them might be comfortable dealing with me directly and not the police."

"This might be harder than you think." Hana grimaced. "I think most non-Drow princess types are a little more bothered by cemeteries than you. I think you're a little too comfortable with creepy stuff there, Goth Princess, even for a magical."

Sonya snorted and laughed, blowing hot chocolate through her nose. She winced before she wiped her face.

"It's not like that." Alison frowned and folded her arms. "Despite my nickname, my favorite color is red! I'm a Drow, not a Goth, and if they're too afraid of a few ceme-teries to keep an eye on them, they should go back home and ask their moms to check their closets for monsters. We need this city to mobilize before it's too late. The police and PDA can't devote all their manpower to tracking body-snatching, even as weird as it is. They don't actually have proof that it's a necromancer or the Tapestry, and they still have all the normal crime and scumbags to deal with. It's time for the underworld to rise out of the shadows and do their part to protect this city from some-thing worse. Considering what happened with Ultimate, they should understand that all too well. And they don't even have to do the hard part of kicking the Tapestry's ass. We'll do that. All they have to do is keep their eyes open."

Hana gave her a thumb's up. "Okay, you've sold me. Let's do this, Dark Princess. Seattle versus the Tapestry. We'll steamroll them."

CHAPTER TWENTY-ONE

"Yo, this is messed up," D-Train muttered from behind the wheel of his car. He sat parked across the street from a small cemetery. The sun had long since retreated, and the settling in of the long shadows of the night left his heart racing. The occasional owl flying overhead didn't do much to slow it down.

He didn't have any issues with a good straight-up fight, but he wasn't down for taking on any zombies. Everyone knew when something crazy happened at a graveyard, it involved zombies. Sure, he'd never seen one or personally knew a person who had, but he'd read about them. He'd even read about how James Brownstone confronted a whole zombie army in Mexico once.

Paulie, a fellow member of D-Train's gang, snorted from the passenger seat. "You heard the same crap we all heard from Franco. The Dark Princess says some assholes are stealing bodies. She wants them found and so many people in the underworld want them found."

"Yeah. That ain't right. But I want some credit with her

if she ever comes knocking our way." D-Train took a deep, cleansing breath. "We can do this shit."

"Why?" the other man asked. "She has a man and he's some jacked life wizard. She ain't going to date your sorry ass."

"Nah. It ain't about that," his companion replied. "I thought about maybe going to work for her."

"Shit, seriously?" Paulie shook his head and scoffed. "So much for oaths."

"Things are different now. We all know it." D-Train grunted. "Even Franco knows it, which is why our asses are out here at night, looking for some creepers stealing bodies rather than slinging at the corner of our territory. Brownstones change shit. Her dad changed LA, and she's changing Seattle. You can pretend that ain't happening, but that ain't going to stop it."

His friend snorted and his face contorted with contempt. "You're tripping if you think she wants someone like you. She won't hire your ass for her company. She don't need no thugs. She needs, like, ex-cops and shit."

"What about the gang members who surrendered to her when she first cleared out the neighborhood around her building?" D-Train countered. "Everyone was talking about that shit."

"What about them?"

"She leveled the ones who tried to attack her, but the other guys, she didn't even turn them over to the cops." D-Train gestured wildly and excitement built on his face. "She gave jobs to some of 'em, including easy ones like keeping an eye on things for her but not doing any enforcement. That's better than the shit I'm doing now." He shrugged. "I'm too old to be slinging on the corner. I could make more money doing practically anything. Franco gets all the money, and we do all the work."

Paulie narrowed his eyes. "You're a damned fool. No one will hire some ex-gang member. You're in for life now, dumbass."

"Why are you even here?" he demanded. "Why do you care about doing something for the Dark Princess, then?"

"I'm only doing this shit because Franco said he would beat anyone's ass who didn't help. But it's because he thinks it's disrespectful and shit to the dead," the other man explained, and his tone made his dismissive opinion clear. "Like I care. Dead people are already dead. Ain't nothing you can do to them that's worse than that."

D-Train frowned at him. "You don't care? Come on. I watched a whole show about this kind of thing. They talked about how Oriceran proves the shit other people have been saying. You can't pretend there's nothing after we die. They know there's more. I even—"

Something dark rushed between two buildings in the distance. D-Train narrowed his eyes and a deep scowl grew on his face. He dropped his hand to the gun tucked into his waistband. "You saw that shit, right? It wasn't only an owl or the trees moving in the wind, right?"

Paulie swallowed and all his sneering confidence evaporated in an instant. "Franco said the Dark Princess only wanted us to observe and report. Snitch without delivering stitches." He fumbled in his pocket and pulled out his phone. "And that's what I plan to do."

His companion scoffed and threw the door open. "I ain't staying here while graverobbers desecrate holy ground. You call, and I'll go stop these sons of bitches." He stepped out and made his way to the fence.

"You'll get yourself killed, dumbass," the other man shouted. "They'll be necromancers and shit."

"Shoot a wizard in the head, and he still dies." D-Train jogged toward the fence. He leapt upward and vaulted over with a firm push with both arms before he landed with a soft grunt. The shadows shifted in the distance again. The gang member hesitated for a moment before he sprinted in that direction, drawing his gun. Two dark forms walked together directly ahead, heading toward the other side of the graveyard. He drew closer to them.

This was his chance. He would prove to Paulie, Franco, and everyone else in Seattle that he didn't need to stay in some tiny gang doing nothing important until the day he died.

The shadows resolved into two plain-looking brown-haired men in dark suits. They stopped and turned to face him, their arms loose at their sides. They didn't have any wands out, and there was no sign of spells around them.

The gang member was disappointed. Even if the typical wizard didn't walk around in a flowing robe and crazy hat, there was something annoying about running into necromancers who looked like accountants.

"The front gate's locked," he announced and licked his lips a little nervously. "So what are you doing here at night? It's mighty suspicious if I do say so myself."

"You are present," one of the men replied, his voice hollow and flat. "Is it not odd for you to question us?"

"I ain't here to cause trouble with dead bodies." He raised his gun. "And I think you are."

"What you believe is irrelevant. You will turn away. You only live because of probabilities."

D-Train's face scrunched in confusion. Now the guy was even talking like an accountant—or, at least, what he believed they might sound like. It wasn't like he actually knew any.

"What the fuck does that even mean?" the gang member shouted. "You want to go? Let's go, necro boy. If you like dead bodies so much, why don't I make you one? But if you think you're too big for old D-Train, what about the Dark Princess?"

The man tilted his head from side to side like a curious bird. "What does Alison Brownstone have to do with you? You are not affiliated with her organization. We know this."

"You got a mouth for a man who ain't even got a gun or a wand out," he snapped. He waved his pistol. "It's too late, assholes. The Dark Princess is coming for your asses, and she'll make you feel the pain. The only reason I'm not popping your ass right now is I'm sure she wants to ask you a few loud questions."

The men looked at each other, and the first one turned back toward D-Train. "Alison Brownstone is coming?"

He grinned and bounced on his feet. The necro accountants didn't sound or look scared, but they wouldn't have asked otherwise.

"Yeah, you creepy-ass dipshits. We already called her. She'll come and drop the hammer on your asses. You disrespected the dead, so she'll disrespect your faces and then turn what's left of you over to the cops."

The men exchanged looks again. A second later, they burst into a quick sprint.

"What the—" D-Train growled and hurried after them, but for every step he took, they drew ahead by two. Their flight brought them to another fence, and they jumped and pulled themselves up and over using one arm.

The gang member slowed, his heart pounding and his hand shaking. Sweat dripped down his forehead, and his lungs screamed.

"It ain't worth it," he wheezed. "Paulie's right. Snitch but no stitch."

Alison yawned as she stepped into the lobby of the Brownstone Building. She'd been so damned close the night before to capturing some Strands. She'd flown directly from her home to the graveyard upon hearing the gang members' report, but the suspects were long gone by the time she arrived, leaving only two shaken low-level thugs and a non-familiar if generic description. Although she did appreciate the colorful name given to the Strands. Necro accountants seemed amusingly appropriate.

The Tapestry harvesters are afraid enough that they can be run off at the mention of my name. Maybe I could simply hire every gang for a few weeks to protect graveyards and shout about how I'm coming. How much could it be? Maybe Latherby could contribute.

A piercing scream shrilled from down the hallway. The receptionist on duty bolted out of her chair and looked in that direction, a hand at her chest and her eyes wide.

No. Damn it.

Alison layered a shield over herself and conjured a shadow blade. She ran toward the hallway. "Containment protocol," she shouted at the receptionist, her heart pounding.

Damn it. I should have known the Tapestry would make their move if they're showing themselves so boldly.

With a shaking hand, the woman entered a series of quick commands into her computer. The shrill wail of alarms filled the air.

"Containment protocol is in effect," Ava's recorded voice announced from hidden speakers. "All non-essential personnel are to immediately evacuate the building."

The receptionist rushed toward the exit, her face ashen.

Another scream sounded. Alison raced down the hallway toward the source. The alarms died.

Have they used an EMP that cut the protocol? Wait. No. The lights are still on.

"Containment protocol is hereby canceled," Ava announced, but it didn't sound recorded. "False alarm. Everyone return to what you were doing."

After a few more steps, she turned the corner and neared the entrance to the pet park. A frowning Ava stood there, her tablet in hand. She stood beside a red-faced Hana, who wore a nervous smile, and Sienna, who cradled a tiny Yorkshire Terrier. They all turned to face Alison.

She skidded to a stop and stared, her blade pointed at the ground. "What the hell is going on?"

"Your spells are unnecessary, Miss Brownstone," Ava announced, and her tone brimmed with annoyance.

"I heard screams," she explained, not willing to argue

with her assistant. She released the energy feeding her shield and sword.

Sienna averted her eyes and drew her dog closer against her. "That was me. I'm sorry."

Hey, someone other than Hana or Jerry is finally using the pet park, but that still doesn't tell me what's going on.

Alison stared at the woman and waited for an explanation.

The junior administrative assistant shuffled her feet. "Look, I love working here, Alison, and you're a cool boss. Even though it's dangerous and all that, the pay is great, and…" She groaned and frowned at Hana. "And it's cool that Hana loves animals so much, but a skunk is totally over the line! Seriously?"

A skunk? What is— Omni became a skunk?

Ava sighed and shook her head. "The skunk has had its glands removed. It couldn't have sprayed you or your dog. Your panic was the result of assumption and ignorance."

"Oh. Removed?" Sienna uttered a nervous little laugh and pulled her dog closer against her chest. "I didn't know you could to that."

Oh, good quick thinking, Ava. A nice, plausible lie.

"Crisis averted?" Alison forced a smile.

Sienna nuzzled her trembling dog. "Alison, can I have a few minutes to take him home? He's all spooked now."

That's because you shrieked like a banshee.

"Fine." She closed her eyes and took a deep breath. Her heart continued to pound. "At least there wasn't actual trouble."

The woman started down the hallway and murmured something about skunks under her breath. She stopped and turned toward Hana. "No offense, but Tahir must be a saint because your house is a zoo." With that, she retreated down the hall with her small mop of a dog.

Alison headed toward Ava and Hana. She peeked inside the open door to the pet park. Omni stood inside, a skunk as Sienna claimed, and poked his head in a cardboard tube. He was brown, as usual, but with white stripes running through his fur.

"A skunk?" She looked at Hana. "I have to agree with her. Seriously?"

The fox shrugged, her cheeks ever redder than before. "It's not like I can control his transformations. He was a ferret when I brought him this morning."

"The problem is that he could have actually sprayed someone." Her forehead wrinkled in confusion. "We have camera coverage on him. How did he change?"

Ava pointed at one of the tubes. "There are plenty of places to hide."

Alison took a few steps into the pet park. She had set up an entire expensive room to hide the identity of one creature, but while it might be easy to explain a concealed ferret, what happened when Omni became a bird who suddenly walked into one end of a tube and came out as a rabbit?

"No more," she declared with a frown.

"What do you mean?" Hana asked, a hint of panic in her eyes.

Alison laughed. "I'm a half-Drow with a royal background. You're a nine-tailed fox, and we have, among other people working for us, a former assassin for the dark families. I think that the rest of the staff won't freak if they know Omni changes shape. They deserve to know why this pet park is here."

Her assistant's jaw tightened. "Do you think it's wise to tell them everything?"

"I think we should tell them the truth. Many of these people have already been through a lot, including the dark wizard attack." She placed a hand over her heart. "I need to start trusting this as much as my head. It's unfair for me to do things that might place the company at risk unless everyone knows what's going on. If I don't trust them, they'll never trust me. The minute I decided to grow this company beyond a handful of people, I lost the right to keep so many secrets."

Ava's expression softened. "I can't say I disagree, Miss Brownstone."

Hana released a sigh of relief. "I totally agree. I want everyone to know how much Omni rocks. For a second there, I thought you were going to tell me we had to get rid of him."

Alison scoffed. "The Tapestry wants him, which is enough reason for us to keep him from them."

"There is the possibility," Ava observed, "that some will be resentful or not want to take the risk of being involved with an unusual creature."

She nodded. "That's true, but at least they'll know. If they want to stop working for me, that's their right. We already know the government doesn't have the balls to take him from us, so there's little reason left to hide the truth. It's not even convenient." She shrugged. "Besides that, I told Latherby about the graveyard incident the other night, and he agreed with me. Our time is running out. It's probably weeks, at most, before the Tapestry makes their move, and it's important that any employee who works for me understands who they are and why they've messed with a few of us in the past."

Omni pulled his head out of the tube and scampered toward a tower of scratching posts.

"How will we tell everyone?" Hana asked.

"Jerry's team finishes that personal protection job today." Alison turned to Ava. "Coordinate a company-wide meeting for tomorrow. I'll brief everyone personally."

"Are you sure, Miss Brownstone?" her assistant asked, an eyebrow raised in question.

"No more secrets from people I claim to trust."

CHAPTER TWENTY-TWO

*S*ometimes, things do work out.

Alison stood in the Brownstone Building lobby and grinned from ear to ear. A crowd had gathered, and dozens of employees chatted as they sipped coffee and ate donuts from the wall of boxes set out on the front reception desks.

She learned toward Ava. "This all worked out even better than I thought it would last week," she whispered. "And thank you for the extra idea. I would have been happy to simply tell them, but your suggestions made it so much better. This went from me not trusting people to a company-bonding moment." She gestured to a large screen hung on the wall.

The text *OMNI WATCH* filled the upper half along with a date range that covered the last week and ended with the current day. Below the main text, different animals were listed, along with names of employees beside them. This screen had been the focus of most people's attention over the last seven days. Now that everyone knew the truth about Omni, it meant they could participate in a fun little game for prizes.

The rules of the contest were simple. Every employee had two votes. They had to choose which form Omni would spend the most time in while he was in the pet park, and they used the second vote to predict the form he would be in on the first hour of the final day of the pool. There were rewards for both predictions, and ties would result in equal prizes. The winners would receive a monetary award along with different gift certificates for restaurants and other local attractions, all arranged by Ava ahead of time and paid for by Alison. No one was allowed to win back-to-back, but that meant someone would be out of the contest only for a week.

Tahir set up a system to automatically catalog the appearance of different Omni forms and displayed them on the board every few hours, so no one would have to worry about spending time tracking Omni. Since only his pet park forms were relevant, it also meant there was no huge advantage for the employees who spent most of their time in the building. To make things fair, Tahir and Hana didn't participate.

"We'll probably need to add a few more categories," Alison suggested. "Maybe something like, 'Form he doesn't ever take during his entire time at Brownstone Security in the week.' Or 'How many distinct mammals does he transform into during a week?' That kind of thing." She scratched her cheek as she pondered the different possibilities.

Ava nodded and entered the notes into her tablet. "That's a good idea. The more variants, the more exciting the game will be for everyone. I don't know how long we can sustain it, but it should provide some diversion for the next few weeks."

"But for now, it's time for our first results." Alison waved her hands. "Can I have everyone's attention?" she shouted.

The cacophony filling the room subsided into a few quiet murmurs and finally, into silence. Everyone turned to face her, expectant expressions on their faces.

She turned and gestured for Hana to enter the lobby. The nine-tailed fox stepped forward, Omni in her arms. He was currently in the form of a brown fox, of all things. Alison wasn't sure if the creature possessed true intelligence and actually played along or if his current form was the universe helping them. Tahir had noted that his diversity of forms had increased in the last month, and so she wondered if the competition had actually had an effect.

Does this have something to do with the Tapestry upping the game as well? He's important to them. Maybe there's some kind of time limitation we don't know about.

The crowd cheered. Omni's head raised and he jumped down to utter a quiet yip before he circled Hana's legs.

"Last week, I shared the truth about Omni with you," Alison announced after the crowd calmed. "And at Ava's insistence, we started this little contest." More cheers followed, and she waited for a few moments. "We had full participation, and I hope everyone continues to have fun with this." She smiled at Ava. "Would you care to announce our winners?"

Her assistant stepped forward. "For our first contest, we have only one winner. This person correctly guessed

Omni's most common form and his form during the first hour of today. The results were cat and iguana, respectively. And our winner is..." She wiggled her finger and pointed. "Jerry."

He grinned and stepped out of the crowd, raised his hand, and nodded to the employees who clapped and cheered around him.

"Congratulations, Jerry," Alison said warmly. "Talk to Ava when everything calms down about collecting your prizes."

The applause continued, and warmth filled her.

Trust is rewarded with trust.

Alison looked up at a knock on her office door. "Come in."

The door opened, and Jerry stepped inside with a smile. "Do you have a few minutes, Alison?"

She gestured to the empty chair in front of her desk. "I was only going through some financials. It's boring, and I'd love any excuse to ignore them." She shook her head. "To be honest, I never thought the company would grow so fast, and having you as the experienced head of the non-magical team is very helpful—more so than I sometimes express. I want to thank you for that."

He closed the door and settled in the chair. The natural gray creeping increasingly into his hair marked him as one of the oldest employees at Brownstone Security, although the way he personally led field teams proved a man didn't need magic to defy age.

"I wanted to touch base with you about this Omni

thing," he explained. "And not only because I'll be able to take my wife out to that restaurant. She's begged me for a while. How did you get reservations?"

"That was all Ava. But what about Omni? It seems like everyone's handling it okay. Am I wrong?"

Jerry shook his head. "I think you did the right thing telling us. I know you like to wall off most of the more dangerous magical stuff, but you should also always remember that every man and woman who works in a field position for this company is ready and able to confront whatever threats that arise." He pointed his thumb at the closed the door. "We wouldn't work for you otherwise."

"I know, and I hope I haven't made it seem too much like the opposite. Some of this is practical." She shrugged. "If your team can make money for the company doing something else while I take the magicals on another job, there's no reason not to. Still, I think we've done a good job to better integrate both sides of the company lately."

"I agree," he replied. "Nothing's changed because of Omni, I want that to be clear."

"I'm a little surprised at how well everyone took everything, especially since the Tapestry is still out there." Alison frowned at the thought and the corners of her mouth settled into a small scowl. "I'm doing my best to not draw anyone into a fight they haven't signed up for."

He chuckled. "I might work for you now, but I'm an ex-cop. Many of my team are, and most people want to do their part even if they aren't ex-cops. Always remember that. We know you'll do right by us, and if we help you eliminate a few extra magicals who abuse their power, I don't think anyone will complain. This is our city, too, Alison." He patted his chest. "I was born and raised in Seattle and some days, I miss being a cop. I miss being able to suit up to protect the innocent from the criminals, but at least here, I can split the difference on most days. It's not always some rich CEO."

Alison's phone rang and she frowned. "That's weird. I thought I set it on vibrate. One sec." She pulled the phone out of her pocket to turn it off but hesitated and frowned at it. The caller ID read, **Take this call; you'll need the help. Seriously.** She narrowed her eyes. "One second, Jerry." She pressed to receive the call. "Hello?"

"Miss Brownstone," said a silky-smooth woman's voice on the other end. "I need to talk to you, and I need to talk to you right away, but it needs to be in private and face-to-face."

"Who is this?" she demanded. "And what is this about?"

"This concerns the neglected arts of weaving," the woman replied. "And the men who focus on them. I'm at the Forbidden Bean at this very moment in a booth near the back. I suggest you come and talk to me. My name is Ophelia, and I can help you with your little Weaver problem. I'll be at the Forbidden Bean for one hour. After that, I will leave."

She snorted. "You expect me to simply show up and talk to someone whom I have never met when you act so suspicious?"

Ophelia uttered a light, merry laugh as if this was the most entertaining thing she'd done all day. The sound made Alison want to punch her in the face.

Okay, calm down. I have no idea who this is. It might be some infomancer screwing with me.

"Consider this a little test, Miss Brownstone," the woman replied. "If we work together, things will sometimes not be on your terms, and that's a little something I think you Brownstones have trouble with. This is as good a time as any to see how flexible you can be. See you soon... or not. It's your choice." She ended the call.

Jerry gestured toward the phone. "Trouble?"

"Maybe, and the clock is ticking. Head to the conference room. I'll call a few other people."

"It's a trap," Mason muttered, his arms folded over his chest. He sat at the large table in the conference room along with Jerry, Mason, Ava, Drysi, and Hana. Tahir had been briefed over the phone as he and Sonya were about thirty minutes away, having left shortly after the contest for some inscrutable infomancer errand concerning enchanted computer components.

Alison shrugged. "I don't know if that changes anything."

"It doesn't change anything that it's screamingly obvious it's a trap?" he pressed. "The Tapestry's trying to make this easy for themselves. The Brownstone Building is protected by so many wards at this point that a frontal assault is more trouble than it's worth, at least while you're still alive. But they obviously assume that if they can pick you off, they'll have a chance."

"Maybe," she replied. "The thought had crossed my

mind, but I'm not convinced. Something doesn't seem right about that explanation."

Drysi stared at the table for a moment as if trying to burn a hole through it with her mind before she raised her head. "We haven't seen any women working for the Tapestry yet. If they are…created, that might explain it." Her nose wrinkled in disgust.

"We haven't seen any directly," Hana interjected, "but that crystal bitch Alison fought had been mutated by True Cores. Maybe this is another crazy witch who worked with Tatum. Or maybe someone who is doing merc work for the Tapestry." She scowled. "Those weirdo graverobbing freaks are getting desperate, and they already proved they'll work with people outside their group."

"That's true," Alison replied. "But I'm still doubtful."

Jerry grunted. "If this Ophelia wanted to assassinate Alison, doing so right next to the Brownstone Building would be a bad idea. And the woman didn't say anything about her coming alone, unlike Tatum's witch."

"Bombs clear groups out," Mason observed.

"Why not simply bomb the Brownstone Building directly?" the other man asked. "I know you have those wards up, but it's not like they'll stop a car bomb."

Mason's expression remained defiant, but he didn't respond.

Ava set her omnipresent tablet down. "If the woman didn't set restrictions, there is no reason to not prepare for a dangerous scenario." She turned her head toward Jerry. "Especially given all the forces available."

He nodded and eagerness lined his face. "You have fifty minutes until her deadline, right? We have almost everyone already here in the building. We can prep full teams and stay at the Brownstone Building until you need us."

"Why don't you go in with Hana and Mason?" Drysi suggested. "I'll stay with Jerry's team, and we can storm the bloody place if needed. We don't want to push in too hard and set her off if she's already a little tetchy. It also means we can defend this place if it's simply an attempt to draw you off for a quick raid."

Alison stood. "Okay, that sounds like a plan. I hope this Ophelia really wants to talk. If not, we'll teach her a lesson about screwing with our neighborhood coffee shop."

CHAPTER TWENTY-THREE

I *hope this isn't an epic mistake.*

Alison pushed into the Forbidden Bean. Every instinct in her screamed for her to summon a shield and a blade and tell everyone to get the hell out of there, but she resisted.

Hana and Mason trailed in behind her. She took a moment to survey the room, looked for people she didn't recognize, and found several, but it wasn't as if everyone who came to the coffee shop was someone she knew. After offering a polite nod to the on-duty barista, she moved deeper into the room and stepped past people sipping on lattes at their tables and reading their phones.

She walked around a corner and entered a small alcove that held two booths. A beautiful dark-skinned woman with short dark hair sat in one. The other remained empty. A steaming cup of coffee stood on a small paper plate in front of her and a half-eaten cinnamon raisin bagel on another plate. The woman looked up, a merry smile on her face, and waved.

Alison paused and stared at her. She looked like she was in her mid-twenties, but nature was no longer the only thing responsible for people's aging. "You're Ophelia?"

The woman nodded and pointed at the leather-upholstered bench seat across from her. "All three of you should fit without too much trouble, or one of you can sit beside me." She winked. "I don't bite. Not without being asked first."

Her attention fixed on the stranger the entire time, Alison made her way slowly to the booth. She slipped into the seat, almost surprised when it didn't explode. Hana took a seat next, but Mason stood directly outside the booth, his hand inside his jacket near his gun and wand.

We shouldn't have a fight in here, but we can't let her get away with anything either.

"You're the dramatic one, aren't you?" Ophelia asked with a grin. "That's fine. Fair warning. I'll reach into my pocket and pull out something small. Don't shoot me, please, even if you are cute, Mr. Lind."

Hana snickered. "She's going after your man, girlfriend. You'd better put a stop to that."

This isn't the time or the place.

Alison glared at her, but the fox shrugged, and her grin grew to match Ophelia's.

Oh, great. I'm glad that at least Hana's entertained.

Mason continued to stare at Ophelia, ready to draw a gun or wand in an instant. There wasn't even the barest hint of amusement in his eyes, only suspicion and anger.

"Go ahead and pull it out," Alison replied. She left one hand on the table but raised her palm. If Ophelia tried anything, she could blast her with a magical bolt in an instant. "Slowly."

"It's kind of funny that you're more paranoid than me," Ophelia replied as she inched her hand into her pocket. "And you'll understand why in a minute." She withdrew her fingers, which now held a small silver cube very similar to another she had seen not all that long before in Ava's hand.

She narrowed her eyes and remained silent until Ophelia set the cube down.

"You're CIA," she stated and made it clear from her tone that it wasn't a question. "Or at least someone with access to CIA tech."

Ophelia tapped the cube. "Ah, good. You already know. You should also know the feed to the cameras pointing at us are being spoofed. We can talk freely about anything without anyone thinking we're talking about anything important. Even if they can read lips, they'll think we had a conversation about the Louper championships."

Alison drew her hand out from under the table and folded her arms over her chest. "You're not simply any CIA, are you? You're part of the Floating City Squad."

The woman laughed. "Floating City Squad? It's been a while since I've heard anyone call us that, but yes." She folded her hands together and her dark eyes twinkled with amusement. "More formally, I'm agent Ophelia Josephine with the CIA Non-Oriceran Alien Task Force."

Mason lowered his hand and some of the tension drained from his face. He took a few deep breaths.

Hana gasped. "CIA? And CIA alien hunter at that? That's so cool."

"It's not cool," Alison insisted. "The last time my family had to deal with CIA alien hunters in a big way, they targeted my dad and mom. They shot my dad with some weird-ass gun that warped reality or something."

Ophelia blew a raspberry and rolled her eyes. "That's all old news. We were both in high school when that happened. And that was Fortis garbage, and your dad finished them before Director Winters started. After that little incident, the few stragglers were easy to mop up. Fortis doesn't exist anymore, not even as a rogue organization. They're past tense."

She scoffed. "So what? The government has tried to screw over my family several times."

"It's also helped you more than a few times. If it weren't for Senator Johnston, your dad would be in some Nine Systems Alliance lab getting dissected."

Alison bolted up, her palms on the table. "You shut the hell up about my dad. If you even come within the same city as him, I'll kill you myself." She growled as if to validate the threat.

Ophelia stared at her and the corners of her mouth curled into a slight smile. "Down, girl. No one wants to lay a finger on the Good Vax. He's the only reason this planet wasn't blown to pieces by his cousins and is probably the main reason why the Alliance isn't trying to annex us and teach us poor natives how to live. Let's be real, Miss Brownstone. I don't know if anyone can stop your father at this point. When Fortis hunted him, it's like you said. They had advanced alien technology, and it only slowed him down. NOAT has better things to do then throw good agents away on an unstoppable alien ass-kicker."

Mason shook his head at Alison, a concerned look in his eyes.

He's right. I don't need the CIA as an enemy if I can help it, but she needs to understand where I'm coming from, too.

Hana watched the exchange and worry lined her face.

"As long as we understand each other," she muttered. "And call me Alison. Something about a CIA agent calling me Miss Brownstone creeps me out." She sank down, her jaw tight. "I'm annoyed. I didn't tell Ava to call you."

Slight surprise played across Ophelia's face. "Ava Garden? I'd love to meet her, but you know what they say about meeting your heroes. Anyway, she didn't call us."

"Then why are you here?"

"Come on." The agent chuckled. "We're not totally incompetent. Things are very different with Director Winters in charge, especially since we have more access to partner technology. It allows us to better monitor unauthorized incursions."

"Partner technology?" Alison snorted. "You mean you're taking crumbs from the Alliance?"

Ophelia shook her head. "Nope. Things are still strained with them. You know, the whole trying to bombard a city on their part, and the whole us not giving them a Vax on our part. They have their reps and what not talking to ours, but I think the last thing they want to give a planet with both a Vax and magic is more tech. We have...other partners. The Alliance aren't the only game in the galaxy, especially because of the relationships Director Winters has cultivated."

Hana beamed. "This is so cool. So the CIA has a bunch of alien tech. It's not in Area Fifty-One, is it?"

"Nope." The woman winked. "I'd tell you where it is but then I'd have to kill you."

"You totally would!"

Mason put his face in his palm and shook his head.

"Can we get back to the actual reason you're here?" Alison muttered.

"The point is," Ophelia explained, "we have a decent ability to monitor for unusual situations due to sharing some of our partners' technology. We constantly monitor in different ways for aliens coming in the back door, if you want to call it that. It's one thing if they want to establish formal, even if secret, relationships with our country, others, or the UN, but we can't have random aliens coming here and starting shenanigans." For the first time in the conversation, something approaching concern appeared on her face. "And there's only so much information we want to get out to the Alliance, too."

"Okay, that all makes sense. So you're saying you've detected alien activity, and it has to do with the Tapestry?"

I'd convinced myself they weren't aliens, but this is all the confirmation I need. A brave new world of annoyance.

The agent nodded. "I'm not really cleared for all the fancy details, and I'm not sure I would even understand them all if they told me, but this area caught our eye when the PDA started asking about this mysterious Tapestry group."

Mason put his hand to his mouth and cleared his throat. "But aliens don't have magic, right? The Tapestry don't use any advanced technology that we've seen and the True Cores are magical. Not only that, but Alphonse Tatum was involved—a wizard."

Alison nodded. "He's right. I thought the whole reason the Alliance was so afraid of Earth was that this was the only planet in the galaxy with magic. We might be connected with Oriceran, but they're not technically in this galaxy and only they can easily get to Earth."

Ophelia wagged a finger. "It's true the Alliance doesn't have magic, and I'll be honest, every other alien species we've ever encountered from this galaxy hasn't demonstrated magic either, but there are no guarantees, right? No one believed in magic for the longest time, even on Earth. More to the point, all that fancy monitoring I mentioned has indicated that there is unusual activity in this area, with that activity suggestive of energy originating from a different dimension." Her forehead wrinkled. "The techies would hate me using that word—maybe plane of existence is better? The point is, someone's visited this area who's not from around here and not from Oriceran, and our little gadgets have swept some of the areas where you've confronted the Tapestry and we've found similar readings."

She leaned back and processed the new information. While she'd suspected in the past that the Tapestry might be aliens, creatures from another dimension came as something of a surprise.

Hana stared at the agent, wide-eyed and her mouth agape. Mason watched the woman, his jaw tight and every muscle in his neck tense.

"Aliens from another dimension," Alison muttered. "Are you serious?"

Ophelia shrugged. "If you were fully cleared, I'd tell you about some of the stuff NOAT has dealt with, both in the couple years I've been with them and all the way back when Director Winters was only a grunt on the ground like me. Sorry, sister, Oriceran is downright boring compared to some of the places eyeing Earth. More to the point, there were two particular spikes of the dimensional energy, or whatever you want to call it. The first was in October and another more recently—shortly after you destroyed the Ultimate ring."

"October?" Alison glanced at Hana, who suddenly looked more nervous than awed.

The agent chuckled. "Let me guess. That's when you found Omni the Wonder Pet?"

The fox offered her a bright smile. "I like you, and I think we can be friends, but I'll fox out and tear out the throats of any CIA agents who try to take Omni."

Ophelia waved a hand dismissively. "Don't worry. Director Winters has made it very clear that we're to maintain, in his words, a cordial relationship with all Brownstones. He's also made it very clear that we won't collect that creature. We wouldn't object if you wanted to…say, hand him over, though."

"That won't happen," Hana snapped.

"Fair enough. I had to ask." She leaned forward and licked her lips. "How do you feel about using him as an alien bloodhound, though? In such a way that we could find and eliminate the Tapestry once and for all? That would make him safer and you all safer as well."

The Brownstone team exchanged glances.

"What are you talking about, exactly?" Alison asked.

Ophelia rubbed her hands together. "This is where we go into an actual plan. The Tapestry wants Omni, and given how you reacted, it's obvious there's a time correspondence between the readings we picked up and when you first ran into him, which means he is probably related to them somehow. Based on what I've been told, we can most likely use the similar dimensional resonance from him to track the Tapestry—kind of like you can normally with a tracking spell."

"They'll come for him eventually," Hana insisted. "I won't hurt Omni to find them."

"Director Winters assured me it wouldn't hurt the little guy." The woman shrugged. "It sounds win-win to me. We can help you destroy the Tapestry and secure this planet from potential invaders, and you won't have to watch your backs so much anymore."

"What do you think, Hana?" Alison asked. "I'm kind of tired of waiting around for the bastards. I had hoped that watching the graveyards would be enough, but if we continue waiting, they might start hurting more innocent people."

The fox sighed. "Do you promise Omni won't be hurt by this tracking?"

Ophelia nodded. "I promise."

Alison frowned. "To be clear, if we help with this, we're helping to the end. Some of my people will be involved. The Tapestry made this personal when they almost killed Hana."

"Understood." The agent's wide grin revealed her dazzlingly white teeth. "Look happier, people. We're probably about to save the world."

CHAPTER TWENTY-FOUR

Ophelia smiled at Omni. The every-pet-in-one lay cradled in Hana's arms in his cat form. He batted at her crystal ring on her hand and meowed.

The two humans stood beside one of the Brownstone SUVs parked in a line in the garage. Drysi sat in the back of the SUV and performed a last-minute check of her daggers while Mason sat in the driver's seat, ready to go. Alison watched Omni, a slightly pensive look on her face.

We can finally end it.

"You don't need an artifact," Hana complained to the cat. "Go hide and get angry."

Jerry and his team members piled into his vehicles. Anti-magic deflectors hung against their vests, rifles were strapped over their shoulders, and their pouches were laden with ammo. Alison had asked for volunteers only, and every member of his team had stepped forward. Brownstone Security was going to war, and this time, they were on the offensive.

"I guess this plan is better than waiting for the Tapestry to blow my house up," she mused and turned to Ophelia. "They won't give me insurance. Did you know that?"

The CIA agent laughed. "I can understand why. You Brownstones do tend to get rowdy."

"It's more that other people come to us and force us to be rowdy."

"Sure." The woman withdrew a translucent frosted glass tube from her pocket. She held it in her palm in front of Hana. "Put this around his neck. I'd do it, but I wouldn't want him to bite me. Whether he's simply a neat pet or an alien who is watching us all, he doesn't know me."

"How am I supposed to get it around his neck?" Hana frowned.

"Bend it."

"But it's glass."

"Don't worry," Ophelia replied. "It'll bend easily enough. Once we get that around him, it should establish a resonance signal that my people can track. I have a NOAT strike team ready to go, and they'll come as soon as the location is confirmed. Even with Director Winters running things, there are certain protocols that need to be observed, especially when working with non-Company personnel." She inclined her head toward a door leading from the parking garage into the main building. "Besides, he feels strongly, given your history, that you should be the one to knock. If there's any chance of doing this without having a huge battle, it'll probably lie in some good old-fashioned Brownstone Shock and Awe."

Drysi snickered from the back seat.

A hungry grin grew on Hana's face. "We'll show those

pet-stealing, drug-dealing, weird-ass extradimensional assholes why they should stay in the Asshole Dimension and leave ours alone—other than sending us adorable strays." She set Omni down and took the tube from the agent. With a quick tug, she verified that it bent as easily as a straw. She knelt and added a new glass collar to her pet. Soft blue light illuminated the tube. Omni purred quietly and rubbed against her hand.

Ophelia tapped her ear. Alison assumed she had some kind of CIA comms device similar to what Tahir had created for her company, but there was nothing visible.

"Understood," the woman murmured. She nodded to Alison and Hana. "They have a signal, and it's close."

"Close?" Alison frowned. "How close?" Her fingers twitched, and she checked the garage for unusual shadows.

Ophelia chuckled. "I only meant it's in Seattle. We can drive there. We don't even have to take a ferry." She walked to the back door of Mason's SUV. "I'll give you directions on the way. It's not really an address kind of thing. I have to point you in the general direction."

"Understood," Alison replied. "Magic tracking often ends up that way."

She slipped into the front passenger seat and slammed the door as Hana got comfortable in the back beside Ophelia and Drysi. Omni curled in her lap with no hint that he knew or understood what was about to happen.

"Time to shred some tapestries," Hana stated with a grin.

Her boss groaned. "Let's not start that nonsense."

The agent laughed. "Why not?" She looked at Hana, a

serious gleam in her eye. "We'll keep tugging on strands until the entire tapestry comes unraveled."

"Keep it up, and I'll flee to their dimension," Alison muttered.

The Brownstone convoy parked about a block away from the target, a long-abandoned mall.

"Tahir, any possible confirmation?" Alison asked.

"There's been considerable peculiar and irregular inter-ference with my drones," he replied.

"Mine, too," Sonya confirmed.

"If we go any lower, we might lose them," Tahir explained.

Here we go, then.

She took a deep breath and willed her racing heart to slow. "It sounds like the kind of Tapestry weirdness we've come to expect," she agreed. "Maintain a high-end view. We have an army here and we'll have CIA support, too, soon enough. You and Sonya stick to the plan and concentrate on making sure that no Strands escape."

Hana stroked Omni's fur. "How can they do that if the Tapestry guys can cancel the feeds?"

Tahir's chuckle sounded smug. "Sometimes, when you're looking for something, you can find it by looking where you can't see it. We have excellent coverage of the area. Any unusual disruptions of feeds will immediately be noticeable, and we can point you in that direction."

"Oh, I get it." She stopped petting Omni to lean over and retrieve the *tachi* sword belt from the floor. The sheath and blade were so long, they stretched across the laps of all three women in the back of the SUV. She tapped her ring, and a red glow spread over her skin. "This will be the most satisfying ass-kicking we've had in a while."

Ophelia nodded at Omni. "It might be best to leave him here. We needed him to track them, but do we want to risk delivering him to them?"

The fox scoffed. "And leave my baby vulnerable to any kidnapping alien out here? The safest place is near us where the Tapestry will have to fight to get him."

Alison shrugged. "I say we bring him. We'll keep the Tapestry busy, and he's good at hiding. If we take him with us, it'll stir them up so they won't try to retreat, and he can hide in a box or something and come out as Angry Omni. We only have to make sure they don't disrupt him, but even if they do, we'll be on them."

Ophelia scratched under his chin and he purred. "I'm not so sure that's a great idea, but as far as NOAT's concerned, we want to destroy the Tapestry unless they're willing to surrender. It's your call."

Mason glanced at the agent in the rearview mirror. "What about local cops? PDA? They never came up in our previous discussions. Shouldn't we have let them know what is going on? We didn't have to admit it involves aliens."

"Nope." She shrugged and a playful smile lingered on her face. "It's harder than you would think to keep aliens a secret in a world where magic exists, and one way to do it is not to invite every law enforcement and federal agent in the area to show up for the big fight with the aliens."

"This won't exactly be a surgical strike," Alison countered. "Once things explode, AET will show up anyway."

"We've taken measures to ensure our privacy during this little shindig." Ophelia winked. "As far as the locals are concerned, we're about to take trouble out of their hands because the government has officially identified the Tapestry as a foreign terrorist group."

"Technically, they are foreign," Hana noted. "And they've done terrorist stuff. So that's not actually a lie."

"Exactly. As long as we keep it contained, the locals won't be involved. And, by the way, everything that's about to happen is classified. I suggest we get going. The sooner we eliminate the Tapestry, the safer the city, country, and world will be."

Alison opened her door and stepped outside. "I'll give them their one chance to surrender, but after that, I'll go all out. I assume that's not a problem? They've never come off as reasonable."

Ophelia shook her head. "Director Winters has made it clear that his only concerns are to discourage any potential invasions and minimize civilian casualties." She slid a hand into her pocket and withdrew a small multi-faceted crystal, which she pressed against her left palm. It began to glow a dull crimson.

"What's that?" Hana asked and leaned closer to peer at the crystal. She sniffed a few times. "I don't smell any magic."

"It's a palm blaster—partner tech. It packs a nice punch but doesn't penetrate. It makes it easy to eliminate the targets without stray shots hitting innocent bystanders on the other side of a wall. You'd be surprised how often dangerous aliens hide in the middle of nice neighborhoods or random shops." She tapped her smart watch a few times.

Mason joined Alison outside the SUV, drew his wand, and cast his standard suite of enhancement spells and shield magic before he holstered it again. He reached for his gun but paused. "We might not actually need anti-magics, will we?"

"Let's see if we can take them down without them. We can always switch." She shrugged.

Drysi moved closer. "What if this goes down like Vancouver?"

Alison gestured at Ophelia with her head. "I assume they have some kind of failsafe, but if the Tapestry had something like that, they would probably have used it already."

The Welsh witch's expression turned concerned. "Sometimes, a bastard doesn't draw his biggest gun until he's trapped in a corner."

"I understand but it's okay. I'll do what I need to do to protect the city." She took a deep breath. "No matter the cost."

Mason frowned at her.

Jerry jogged over from his SUV and the anti-magic deflector bounced lightly against his vest. "We're ready to move, Alison." His squads clustered around their vehicles, dozens of men and women ready to go.

"My team will knock on the front door," she replied. "When we enter the location, we'll need squads to cover all the exits. I don't want any of these freaks to escape. This ends today."

"Understood."

Hana strapped her sword belt on, and Omni circled her, meowing plaintively.

Maybe he's eager to get going and eat some Strands. Cats like threads.

"Let's do it." Alison layered shields over herself and conjured a shadow blade.

Although she wanted Jerry's team to cover the other exits and had Tahir watching, she wasn't all that worried about the Tapestry running. After all, she had brought Omni to them. She didn't worry that it was a mistake, given the strike force that had accompanied her.

Jerry's team kicked into a quick jog and fanned out into smaller squads on either side, their rifles at the ready.

Dad did the same thing. He had the government backing him up in LA. He might have taken on the Vax himself, but Senator Johnston, the military, and the PDA kept the Alliance off his ass. I guess it's not always bad to have a little official backup.

"These guys weren't that bad last time," she noted. "They only overwhelmed Hana because they surprised her when she was unarmed, and she still managed to kill a fair number of them."

"It'll take me a while to enchant replacements for all the bloody daggers I'm about to use," Drysi mumbled.

"I think we'll all deserve a long vacation after this one," Mason suggested.

"Maybe we'll do exactly that," Alison replied.

Ophelia tapped her watch. A bright yellow translucent energy shield extended in front of her arm. "We don't usually have magicals of your power level to back up our field teams, nor even the numbers you've brought with your secondary teams. I'm sure we'll do fine. It might even be a little fun."

Hana patted the hilt of her *tachi*. "It was bad enough when they were simply petnappers. Now I know they're alien invaders, too. I can't wait to stop these jerks."

The group approached the parking lot of the mall. A massive pulsating white dome appeared with a hum and encircled the entire area.

Okay, we're already surprised. We're not off to a great start.

"What the hell is that?" Alison shouted.

The agent waved a hand and looked chagrined. "Oh, sorry. Don't worry. That's us."

"All personnel, ignore the white dome," she transmitted through her comms. She pointed at the sphere. "For something you want to keep classified, you've gone out of your way to draw considerable attention to it."

"Nope. It's simple. Everyone outside the dome and even satellites checking infrared bands only see the mall, but it's not an actual forcefield. It won't keep any fleeing Strands inside. It's mostly there to make it easier for us to explain this all away later."

Waves of energy rippled through the dome.

Alison lowered her head and turned toward Mason. "Do you feel any extra magic?"

He shook his head.

Hana sniffed the air. "I smell the magic from you and our artifacts but nothing from the dome."

"Oh, that's partner tech, not magic," Ophelia explained. "We do have magicals in NOAT, but we still tend to rely on toys more than spells."

"Technomagic, alien tech, genetic engineering…" Alison

began and shrugged. "The Earth will be way, way different a hundred years from now. It won't even be recognizable."

Jerry's squads disappeared in the distance as they fanned out around the building to where small groups set up outside the exits. Each reported the same thing. The doors were all boarded up and covered with black plastic from the inside. The same was true of the six-door main entrance when Alison and her team arrived.

The Tapestry is stealing bodies and hiding out in dead malls. Somehow it all seems appropriate.

She released her shadow blade. "You said Winters wants me to knock, right, Ophelia?"

The CIA agent's eyes widened. Her mouth parted in obvious excitement. "You don't have to hold back." She winked. "If there's one thing the CIA is good at, it's lying to the American people."

Alison raised her hands and took a deep breath before she channeled magic between her hands to grow an explosive orb.

Aliens. Drow. Dark wizards. On some days, I think Christie has the right idea.

The CIA agent took a few steps back together with Mason and Drysi. Hana looked around with a frown.

"Where did Omni go?" she asked.

"That's good, isn't it?" Ophelia replied. "He can go into a dumpster and come out a blender-monster, right?"

The fox sighed. "I guess. I kind of wanted him to see Mommy kick the aliens' asses first." She drew her sword. "But maybe we'll get lucky and the Tapestry will surrender."

My city. My responsibility.

Alison slowed her breathing as she continued to funnel magic into her orb, which grew steadily brighter and larger.

Mason put his gun away and drew his wand again. "Be careful, A."

"We're not the ones who need to be careful," she replied. "Knock, knock." She released her attack.

CHAPTER TWENTY-FIVE

The orb rocketed away from Alison and crackled with power as it pounded into the entrance. The massive explosion consumed the doors and overhang and a plume of smoke, glass, plastic, and concrete erupted. The smoke began to clear after a few seconds. A partial crater marred the front of what remained of the entrance, filled with piles of concrete littered with smoldering debris. An abandoned food court along with a long-dry fountain lay beyond the devastation. Two stationary escalators now served as silver stairs leading to an empty second story.

Hundreds of brown-haired almost identical men in dark suits choked the food court. Their eyes were all solid black and darkened veins ran through their faces and necks. They didn't move a muscle as they stared directly ahead.

"It looks like they already downed their True Cores," Alison muttered. "And that's more Strands than last time." She tapped her ear to transmit. "All teams prepare to breach. We have a higher number of the enemy than expected but wait for my signal."

A single man stepped forward. "Alison Brownstone." He jerked his head as his gaze traveled from person to person and finally lingered on Ophelia. "You are unknown to us, even as Weavers. You are not a normal ally of Alison Brownstone."

She bowed with a smirk. "That means I'm doing my job. Agent Ophelia Josephine, US Central Intelligence Agency, Non-Oriceran Alien Task Force. You are violating American territory, and your leaders have not previously contacted anyone in our government, which means you've violated all kinds of policies we have in place. This doesn't have to go down poorly, despite the fact that you have already attacked American citizens and are"—she grimaced —"stealing our bodies."

"Your kind no longer has need of them," the Weaver replied, his expression neutral. "You cannot express such disdain."

Drysi scoffed. "Cheeky bastard, isn't he?"

"So you admit you made them into Strands?" Alison shouted. "Is that what all of you are? Nothing but recycled bodies?"

He shook his head. "Living material is preferred to conversion, but too many have been watching. Your personal efforts have damaged our forces to an unexpected degree."

She shuddered. "Living material is preferred? You've killed innocent people, you sons of bitches."

"These bastards make the Seventh Order look nice," Drysi murmured.

The Weaver tilted his head and regarded Alison with the habitual blank expression she had come to loathe. "If we take a few from many places, it is easy. Your planet has an excess of humans. It did not harm you. In fact, you did not even know."

Hana's claws grew and her tails appeared. Her vulpine eyes filled with hatred. "You're disgusting."

"Pumping your dead with chemicals and not reclaiming their base materials or incinerating them is inefficient," he replied. "But this is all irrelevant. We can sense that the target is near. You have not been attacked only on the small probability that you have brought the target to surrender it to us."

"I'll die ten times before I let you assholes lay one finger on Omni," the fox growled.

The Weaver nodded. "One death will be sufficient." He turned his gaze toward Alison. "Is this your position as well, Alison Brownstone?"

"My plan is to make sure you all die before any of us do, but sure, the sentiment is the same." She summoned a new shadow blade and offered her best impression of an evil grin. Maybe she could intimidate them.

"We acknowledge your position despite its irrationality." He focused on Ophelia next. "You represent the government of this nation state. It is illogical to punish us for our incursion when Alison Brownstone and Hana Sugimoto are protecting a dangerous creature that could harm humans if left unchecked. Hand it over to us, and we could take that under consideration."

"Are you saying you want to make some kind of deal?"

Ophelia asked and the light of her energy shield danced across her face.

"Offers can be made," the Weaver suggested. "Your nation state can be spared and allowed some autonomy once our plan is complete."

The agent's dark eyebrows raised. "Now that sounds like a threat. Who are you really? Don't feed me any crap. We already know you're not from this galaxy, and we know you're not from Oriceran. You're from some kind of different dimension. Why are you here? Why the weird name?"

He didn't speak for several seconds and instead, simply stared at her. "We are tools of something greater, the Source. All names have power, especially in the home of the Source, but also here. They crystalize concepts into something concrete. A concept becomes a sound, and the sound becomes existence. His world is different than yours, less physical. The Source reached out to find a concept that would bind his will into physical forms and allow us stable existence in this physical world to serve his will."

Alison frowned. "Why are you suddenly telling us all this?"

"There is a small but non-zero probability that it might persuade you to agree to our plans. Our calculations indicate that otherwise, a battle will be launched and unnecessary resources will be lost."

I'm not sure if that means he's overconfident or he's afraid.

"Who is the Source?" Ophelia asked and her voice wavered slightly.

"Our creator," the Weaver replied with hesitation

although his voice remained as emotionless and flat as before. "The Source's will and essence fills his entire world and binds it in peaceful unity. There can be no conflict where there is no individuality. No suffering where there is no want. If all give themselves to the Source, the Source will become all. You should not resist us. We are the extension of the Source in your world. We can bring your world peace and then your galaxy peace."

Alison snorted. "So that's your grand plan for our future? For everyone to become mindless drones of some alien god like you?"

He shook his head. "You don't understand. The Tapestry are a tool, nothing more. The Source cannot manifest directly in this world yet as the nature of your physical reality still necessitates individual forms for our work. We are inefficient tools and not representative of the Source. There is still too much individuality in our forms. We must continue the experiment and provide a vessel as a seed. Thus, experiments are necessary, even if physical bodies are crude and inefficient. The creature you protect is critical to our experiments and as a vessel. Your nation state does not have to be an enemy of the Tapestry or the Source. Give the creature to us, and some level of autonomy can be maintained. If you do not cooperate, the Source will likely punish others for your mistakes. Your nation state is unnecessary and harbors potential elements that might resist his efforts. Prove that it should not be destroyed."

Alison uttered a dark chuckle. "You don't really understand the whole carrot and stick idea, but nice try. You've done nothing but be hostile toward us the entire time. You almost killed Hana."

"She brought that on herself by resisting us. The creature was never hers to defend. We need it to finish our experiments and provide a physical template the Source can use for entry." The Weaver straightened his head. "We were forced to take what is ours. What is the Source's. One creature's life is irrelevant before that possibility."

She scowled at him. "You stole bodies by your own admission, killed other people by your own admission, and even if I bought into your weird alien reasoning, you teamed up with a dangerous criminal to enhance other criminals with Ultimate. I assume that was another kind of experiment, but I don't care."

"You cannot blame us for the existing problems in your atomized society. The Tapestry's actions would end those problems. Taking advantage of existing weaknesses is only logical."

"You put this city and country at risk, and you've already stated that your intentions are to effectively conquer this planet and the galaxy. Do you seriously think we'll agree to help you?"

The Weaver shook his head. "No, calculations indicated a minimal probability of success."

Alison took a deep breath and looked at Ophelia. "Have you heard enough?"

She raised her hand with the palm blaster and covered the rest of her body with her shield. "Yes."

The alien tilted his head from side to side a few times. "You should consider the probabilities of your own success or lack thereof before you commit to any irrevocable actions."

"You already told us you plan to take control of our planet," Alison replied. "What good does it do to even listen to you?"

"The Source will spread from the Earth to other worlds. It might be necessary to have some independent entities remaining to serve as the Source's agents in some circumstances. We can allow your nation state's people to serve in that role."

Hana rolled her eyes. "And you expect us to believe you?"

He looked at her without expression. "Evaluate the probabilities. If the Source takes your world and then your galaxy, your nation will fall anyway. A small but non-zero probability of our bargain being kept is still higher than the zero probability that you will be able to resist the combined might of an entire world unified as one being. You will perish and accomplish nothing for your efforts."

Alison snickered. "I almost pity you assholes. You don't even understand how to negotiate with us in good faith, but it doesn't matter." She lifted her blade. "The last time we fought, we destroyed most of you, and we didn't have my other teams with me, let alone CIA alien hunters." She grinned at Ophelia before she returned her attention to the Weaver. "Sure, you have more Strands this time, but it's merely more people to eliminate. This is your last chance to stand down, because as far as I'm concerned, you just announced an alien invasion of our entire galaxy and maybe our universe, and I won't surrender because of some half-assed promise to turn the US into your servants."

The Weaver gave her a curt nod in response. "Is this also the position of the United States Central Intelligence Agency?"

Ophelia nodded at her shield. "This should be your answer. NOAT considers you hostile invaders and will react with all due force to defend America's territory and citizens."

"Very well, then. You are both foolish. We would not confront you if we hadn't improved ourselves since our last encounter. You are a threat. You will die and we will take the creature. The Source will come to Earth, and your world will become the Source."

Alison drew her blade back and prepared to attack. "We'll see about that."

CHAPTER TWENTY-SIX

"Jerry, go," Alison transmitted. "Withdraw immediately if you can't handle it."

The Strands surged forward, their movement a blur with no fear, no concern, and no anger. They were nothing but a dark tide, a force of nature. There was something almost insulting about them not showing any emotion.

A shimmering orange-red orb careened from Ophelia's palm and exploded against the Weaver to vaporize the front half of his body. His corpse fell and sizzled. Drysi flung two red daggers into the approaching line. The blast launched several burning bodies into the air. Mason joined the fun with a few fireballs of his own. Alison flung several quick shadow crescents that sliced the Strands in half.

I thought he said they were tougher than before, but they're going down easily. It must be about overwhelming us with numbers.

Hana brought her sword up and waited as two Strands rushed toward her. Two quick slices removed their heads.

All the improvements of the True Cores couldn't do much for a head without a body.

Ophelia fired several more shots and felled her targets, her eyes narrowed in concentration. For all her jokes and lightness, she clearly took the fight seriously.

The combined attacks of Drysi, Hana, Mason, and Alison carved into the Strand front line, but new enemies filled the holes immediately. The roiling tide moved inexorably forward like the ocean pounded the beach and threatened to overwhelm the small force.

The sound of glass shattering echoed in the distance. Heavy rifle fire followed.

"There's Jerry," Alison shouted. She summoned twin shadow blades and spun to carve into three surging Strands.

Ophelia hissed as an enemy swung at her. She held it off with her arm shield before she obliterated the top half of his body with a point-blank shot. "Sorry about the delay. My backup will be here. We merely have to survive until then. No pressure, right?"

Drysi screamed something in Welsh as she delivered several of her red daggers in rapid succession. The far flank of the Strand line disappeared in a curtain of raging flame and acrid burning cloth and flesh. Mason holstered his wand and met an approaching attacker with his fist. The enhanced blow cracked against the man's head and catapulted him into others that raced forward toward him. They caught and tossed their wounded comrade to the ground and trampled him as they continued their attack with no concern for the dead around them.

Alison hurtled forward and swung her twin blades

methodically. The sheer number of enemies gave her no time to think, let alone channel something more powerful. If she flew, she might be able to accomplish it, but she'd leave Ophelia, Hana, Mason, and Drysi vulnerable.

It'd be nice if Angry Omni showed up.

Rifles cracked in the distance, the muzzle flashes visible behind the massive army of Strands.

The density of the crowd lessened. Some of the adversaries near the back broke away and ran in opposite directions, most likely to deal with the advancing non-magical squads. The nearby horde punched and clawed at Alison. Their blows strained her shields and stung but none penetrated. Every Strand who landed a strike ended up headless or stabbed through the chest a moment later. The bodies began to pile up around her.

Hana bounded from Strand to Strand and carved through them with ease. Their blood splattered in every direction from the power of the *tachi* unleashed with the speed of the nine-tailed fox.

Drysi reached into her vest and cursed. Her early efforts had been effective, but she was now out of daggers although she'd effectively obliterated dozens of the enemy. A quick yank of her wand and a shout conjured a fireball that added another victim to her list. Mason grunted as he landed several more blows and caved in the skulls of a few new arrivals.

None of them are regenerating, Alison thought. *Did they need time to improve them after their graverobbing?*

A mass of new Strands clambered over the bodies surrounding Alison and snapped her attention back into the battle. She hacked away at the new forces.

Ophelia took advantage of a brief lull in attacks against her to draw a small clear glass sphere from her pocket. She squeezed it and lobbed it behind the front line of the Strands. A bright white pulse of energy discharged from the point of impact and covered a dozen nearby hostiles in a thick layer of ice. They collapsed with a combined thud and formed a small ice wall that forced at least a few to vault over.

More enemies hurtled toward the CIA agent before she could deploy another toy. Sweat beaded her forehead as she fired into them and incinerated one after another. Their horrendous losses didn't seem to change their strategy or display as any visible concern on their faces.

"This is damned endless," she muttered.

The shouts and gunfire grew closer in the distance.

At least we have something approaching a pincer movement.

Some of the earlier casualties began to sizzle and their bodies and clothes slowly disintegrated.

Alison spun in a circle—a crude tactic, but she didn't run out of targets for a good ten seconds. She leapt back after she'd eliminated the Strands, her breathing ragged.

The enemy forces were beginning to thin. Their efforts had reduced the massive choking horde down to a more manageable killer mob.

Drysi shouted almost continuous incantations. Her fireballs pounded their adversaries relentlessly. None of the enemy could get within ten yards before she annihilated them.

Mason slammed his elbow into the face of one man before he delivered a roundhouse kick as a follow-up. His enhanced speed made his spin almost a blur, and the crack of impact could be heard even over the echoing gunfire.

Alison sprang back even farther and released her swords. She alternated thrusting her hands forward to launch a steady stream of light bolts into the enemy line. Strands fell in rapid succession, their chests burned.

Her heart thundered, but not from the battle. Something didn't seem right.

Is it a trap? Do they plan to blow the building up? I don't sense that kind of magic.

She tried to ignore the thought as she continued her rapid-fire magical barrage. Five seconds. Ten seconds. A screaming Hana bisected a Strand with her sword. Ophelia hurled another sphere. The new one transformed a half-dozen of the enemy into black dust.

With the assault slowing, Drysi switched from fireballs to pulling barriers out of the floor to form a natural funnel into a kill zone for the advancing Strands.

"Pull back, Hana!" Alison shouted.

The fox growled and scampered back, her tails flowing behind her. Whatever speed the True Cores granted, it wasn't enough for them to keep up with her.

The Strands didn't even try to dodge as they entered the kill zone. Overlapping fire from Drysi, Alison, and Ophelia converged, supplemented by a now wand-wielding Mason who added his own bolts. The volleys shredded and burned the charging aliens. A minute later, there was no enemy left to kill. The gunfire had died down, and she could make out her employees on the far end of the cavernous mall.

Alison took several deep breaths before transmitting. "Jerry, status?"

"There were more than we expected, Alison," he replied. "We have a few injuries but nothing serious, but we're damned low on ammo. We switched to anti-magics, but it didn't seem to make a huge difference. Even with those, we had to put a lot of bullets into one to kill them."

"Pull back to the SUVs," she ordered. "It looks like we have the situation under control, and we have additional backup coming soon. Your team can't do us any good without ammo, anyway."

"Okay, we'll pull back," Jerry replied.

"Tahir?" Alison asked. "Are you there?"

"You have two dropships that just landed near the front," he replied. "They appeared out of nowhere—probably some kind of full-spectrum camouflage or spell."

"That doesn't sound like the Tapestry's style." She turned toward Ophelia. "Did your friends just arrive?"

The CIA agent nodded and offered her an apologetic smile. "They always leave me to do the hard work."

"I know the—" Alison refreshed her shields with a fresh infusion of magic and pointed at the second floor. Scores of Strands now filled that level, but unlike the fast, tough, but ultimately disposable enemies the team had fought, these would not fit in at the local coffee shop.

Each was unique in his own way. One man's hand ended in sharp claws. Jagged bone-like growths protruded from the skin of another. Razor-sharp teeth filled the mouth of a third. A blue nimbus surrounded a Strand, and he wasn't the only one with an obvious shield.

Ophelia snickered. "It looks like they finally sent in the varsity squad."

Alison immediately shunted power into growing an energy lance. The white mass of magic grew in front of her and dark strands of shadow magic swirled around it.

A dozen suited CIA agents ran in from behind, a bizarre mirror of the Strands. Pulsing white forcefields surrounded each of the men and women, and they all held long silver rifles with barrels far too thin to fire any normal bullets.

They attacked immediately and the weapons fired thin blue beams that seared through their targets and what remained of the escalator and sections of the second floor. The agents swept the barrage across the enemy ranks and the force ripped several of the new Strands to shreds but left some completely unharmed. Several of those with glowing shields absorbed the attacks.

The Strands began to leap from the second floor and barreled down the damaged escalators. Alison released her spell. It exploded against the top of one of the escalators and scattered several of the attackers. Combined with the CIA's effort, she'd removed most of the escalator and turned the top into enough of a smoking ruin to force several of them to jump, which left them open for more attacks from the gathered CIA and Brownstone teams.

If these guys get near us, they'll probably carve half the team up.

She gritted her teeth as she forced even more power into two dark orbs.

The CIA's guns—no doubt partner technology—continued to slice through most of the remaining Strands.

The man with the blue forcefield landed and rushed toward them, his face as expressionless as the others' despite the piles of dead and disintegrating allies that filled the area. The CIA agents, including Ophelia, tried to concentrate their fire, but his shield held.

Hana sprang forward and swung the *tachi* at his neck. The blade passed through the shield and decapitated him. His body managed to clear a few more yards before gravity won the battle.

Alison released her orbs at other shielded adversaries. The orbs hammered into them and their energy fields disappeared. Drysi, Mason, and the CIA agents followed up with a volley that carved the now vulnerable enemies into pieces.

Everyone jerked their heads around in search of more enemies or for any sign of movement.

"There were failures in calculations," a booming voice intoned. Another suited man advanced to the edge of the burning second floor near the top of the mostly destroyed escalators and the smoldering pile of rubble. He stared at Alison, his eyes solid black but his mouth curled down into a faint hint of a scowl.

So we finally did enough to piss one off, huh?

CHAPTER TWENTY-SEVEN

The CIA agents fired at the man, but the rays struck an invisible shield a few inches from his body. Drysi and Mason both attempted rapid shots with fireballs, but they exploded against his shield and did no more harm than the CIA's tech marvels. Alison tried a light bolt followed by a shadow crescent, but neither attack even ruffled the man's jacket.

He leapt down from the second story and landed with surprising grace. "It doesn't matter. The target remains nearby even if you have forced our hand. The time is short. As long as we recover the target, the loss of resources is irrelevant."

Alison snorted. "We? The rest of your allies are gone, asshole. We'll get through your shield."

"We are the Overseer," the new arrival explained.

"Does that mean you're in charge of the Tapestry?"

"We are the first among equals," he replied. "The resource sacrifice is unfortunate, but it gave us enough time to further understand the nature of our enemies and make appropriate adjustments."

"Meaning what?" Hana shouted. She pointed her blade at him. "Your other guys thought they were immune to everything until they met my friend here. Why don't you come a little closer? I'll offer you a little education in Japanese weapons history." She pointed to a pile of half-disintegrated Strands. "You can join them. First among equals and all."

The Overseer shook his head. "We cannot fail. You will not stop us."

Ophelia rolled her eyes. "There's nothing worse than a stubborn jerk. You've lost, Overseer. Your army is gone, and unless you have another container of suit zombies to fling at us, it's all over." She gestured around. Many of the earliest casualties had already disappeared, clothes and all, and most of the others were well on their way.

"No. Taking full advantages of flaws in the nature of this local physical reality will allow you to be defeated." The Overseer tilted his head and stared at Alison. "My continued existence is irrelevant to completing the plan."

She narrowed her eyes when she sensed magic pulsing from the Overseer, even above the heavy background levels.

Mason and Drysi both frowned. Hana's nose wrinkled.

"What are you doing?" she asked.

"Giving of myself to complete the plan," he explained and raised his arms.

"Get down!" Alison shouted.

A massive wave of black energy surged from him. She blinked as it passed through her. It didn't hurt her or strip her shields. Her skin tingled, but it wasn't an uncomfortable sensation. Something clattered on the floor behind her.

She laughed. "That's it? Not impressive." She turned to look at Hana, and her breath caught. The sound she had heard was the *tachi* hitting the floor.

Hana, Mason, Drysi, and Ophelia, along with all the CIA agents, lay on the ground and groaned. All the barriers the Welsh witch had conjured were gone, replaced by piles of dust.

"What the hell?" She turned back toward the Overseer, her stomach knotted.

Shit. I underestimated him.

He tilted his head in the strange way all the Strands did. "We are not surprised you were not defeated, Alison Brownstone. You are touched directly by two worlds, and it's harder to make the appropriate adjustments because of that. But now that your allies have been defeated, I will kill you and your genetic resources will be added to the efforts of the Tapestry. You will live on to serve the Source. You may have defeated the others, but we are the combination of several Strands. We will defeat you, even at the cost of hastening our own end."

She snorted. "You couldn't even knock me down with your big ultimate attack, and now you talk about beating me? Aren't you getting ahead of yourself?" She didn't want her concern over her friends to show.

The Overseer's mouth twitched, then his head and arms. A tremor rippled through his entire body and barbed tentacles burst from his sides and legs.

Alison wrinkled her nose. "That is not a good look."

The suit thickened into a tough dark-brown hide, which continued to harden and change texture. Plates overlapped one another until it was more a carapace than a skin or hide. His legs grew. Several sprang from the bottom of his body, along with more tentacles. Mouths filled with sharp, pin-like teeth appeared on the lump that had once been the top of his body. Solid black eyes also opened all over the length of his upper torso. He continued to change until he was a massive dark-brown, twenty-foot-tall alien monstrosity that towered over her on nine legs. His tentacles writhed and twitched, the barbed tips suffused with a soft green light. His many mouths twitched. No one would have ever known the monster had once been humanoid.

"Not quite what I expected, but if I won against a Mountain Strider, I can win against you," she declared but swallowed with genuine trepidation. She layered a few more shields around herself. "You're still a living thing, and all living things can die."

An unsettling multi-tonal keening erupted from the mouths of the Overseer.

"That's about the worst thing I ever heard in my life. Okay, time to end this."

Alison thrust her palm forward and launched a light bolt. It struck the tubular mass that passed for the Overseer's body and dissipated into nothingness. She followed up with a shadow crescent. A thick green fluid poured from the resulting laceration, but the wound sealed itself in a few seconds.

"Regeneration, huh? All I have to do is slice you into enough pieces to win, I suppose." She extended a shadow blade and narrowed her eyes. Shadow wings emerged from her back, and she took to the air and circled the Overseer. A quick dive brought her close to him, and he slapped at her with a tentacle. It sliced easily through her shield and ripped into her flesh.

She hissed in pain and rocketed upward. Blood seeped from the wound.

The chorus of mouths announced, "You're not immortal either, Alison Brownstone."

Loud thudding footsteps sounded from behind her.

Oh, shit. Now what?

Alison turned, and a massive form, easily matching the height of the transformed Overseer, stood behind her barely conscious teammates.

Like the Overseer, the creature had a dark-brown, hard outer covering, but unlike the eldritch monstrosity in front of her, this new creature seemed strangely more comprehensible. Four arms ended in sharp claws, and four dark eyes stared out of his flat and almost triangular head, his thin mouth almost invisible. The pattern continued with his four thick legs, but at least he only had a single tail. The creature tilted its head and looked at Hana before he uttered a loud hiss at the Overseer.

"Wait a minute." She laughed. "I didn't recognize you because you had extra arms and legs and are so big." She turned toward her adversary. "You've really done it now, asshole. Your people dealt with Angry Omni and now, you have to deal with Jumbo Angry Omni."

"Impossible," the chorus of mouths bellowed. "The target cannot have self-actualized to such an extent."

She floated closer to Omni and kept her back to him

and her eyes on the tentacled Overseer. "I don't know much about how your freaky little group works or your creator, but you've told me enough that I understand you aren't really individuals, and that's unfortunate. If you were and you actually had some damned emotions, maybe you could understand about how caring about something— actually caring—can make a difference." She summoned another blade. "Let's finish this, Omni, for Hana."

He hissed and charged, his arms raised. The Overseer screeched from every mouth as he batted at his new foe. His sharp tentacles sliced at the thick armor that protected the transformed every-pet. Omni responded with rapid swipes of his claws and ripped chunks of flesh from his enemy.

Alison used her opportunity to dive toward the alien and sliced her shadow blades at the base of the tentacles. She severed three in a quick pass before she spun to avoid a few others when they counterattacked. Omni's claws dug deep into their opponent while she circled for another strike.

Some of the Overseer's wounds began to seal and the stumps of his cut tentacles began to grow, but her next pass removed even more appendages. Her giant partner's relentless efforts continued to gouge massive wounds in the alien. When the first beating green mass emerged, Alison knew how to win, especially since the rents in the Overseer's side revealed several more of the same green masses.

I knew this asshole had multiple hearts, even if they're all mutated now. That makes sense if he's actually multiple Strands joined together.

Several tentacles wound around Omni's arms and pinned them to his sides. He hissed in anger and thrashed wildly.

She flew toward the rapidly closing wound, hacked at some of the exposed hearts, and managed to cut one out. The monster writhed in pain. Omni freed an arm and tore the offending tentacles off, including those holding his other arm.

The Overseer stumbled back, his movements now uneven, and the tentacles twitched slower than before. Omni alternated with his claws to grate and rasp the already wounded alien's chest.

Wait. He has him opened like he's about to do surgery.

Alison released her blade and began to fling shadow crescents directly into the exposed hearts. Without the exterior armor, the missiles sliced the organs in half and produced a shower of green blood. The next thirty seconds seemed incredibly long to her, even as she worked with Hana's pet to destroy each heart left in their mutual foe.

The monster collapsed onto its back and a faint hiss escaped all his mouths. "I will simply regenerate, Alison Brownstone. Even if you do defeat us, we will return. The Source is patient. Your years are nothing. Your decades are nothing. Your centuries are nothing."

"Omni, back off," she commanded. "I'll finish this." She threw her arms to the side and shadow and light magic flowed together into dozens of small dark-speckled white energy spheres that orbited her as she hovered in the air.

Omni hesitated for a moment and hissed his anger before he backed away and positioned himself in front of Hana.

"If more Strands come back in a few centuries, the average little kid on the street will probably be powerful enough to kick your ass. But keep the dream alive. Goodbye for now." She lowered her arms.

The spheres careened forward and pelted the Overseer. Each detonated into a mass of purple flame that incinerated the flesh around it. Several seconds passed before the deadly barrage finished and left only a few twitching tentacles that soon stilled and a pile of disconnected legs, a scorched, shallow crater between them.

Alison lowered herself slowly to the ground and watched the remains for any sign of regeneration.

"Tahir?" she asked. "Are you there?"

Silence greeted her.

The stupid wave attack must have shorted our comms. More money to spend.

She folded her arms and tapped her foot as she continued to stare at the body. There was no sign of regeneration.

"That has to be about the weirdest damned thing I've ever killed," she announced. "Right, Omni?" She turned and laughed.

The four-legged behemoth killing machine was gone, replaced by a tiny brown panda that nuzzled a groaning Hana.

Ophelia sat up, her hand to her forehead. "We'll have a few gnomes mark their planners."

Alison blinked. "Huh?"

"I couldn't move but I could still hear everything. The Overseer said all that crap about coming back." The agent shrugged and winced. "We'll pencil a reminder for gnomes.

'Remember weird-ass alien attack a few centuries from now.'"

"I'm glad to see you have the important priority of thinking up witty comebacks when we fight off an alien invasion."

Ophelia managed a weak grin. "Hey, that is important. Those guys didn't seem to like jokes. Maybe humor is our ultimate weapon."

"It could be," she replied.

Mason pushed himself up and took a deep breath. Soon, Drysi and the other CIA agents were at least seated.

Hana rolled onto her back and sighed. "Is it finally over?"

The Overseer's body began to disintegrate.

"I hope so."

CHAPTER TWENTY-EIGHT

Alison leaned against the side of her SUV. They'd reestablished contact with Tahir, and he and Sonya hadn't seen any indication of Strands fleeing, directly or otherwise. Mason and Drysi had tended to the injuries among Jerry's team. The only reason no one had left was because Ophelia asked them to stick around for a while until the CIA finished with a few things, along with making them all individually give their oral agreement to keep the events they had participated in secret.

Hana sat on the ground, her back against the car and the baby-panda-sized Omni in her lap. "Is it weird that I am never freaked out by this kind of thing anymore? Before I met you, a bad gangster attack would have spooked me. Now I fight aliens, dark wizards, and crazy-ass wizard mad scientists. And half the time, I think it's fun."

"I don't know if that means you're brave or desensitized," Alison admitted. "But at least we help to protect this city."

"Being a con artist seems like fifty years ago." The fox gave Omni a quick squeeze. "But I don't think I miss it."

Ophelia approached them with a coy smile. "Thanks, Alison. I'll admit that at first, I thought we would have to do all the heavy lifting, but we would have had our asses handed to us without you and Omni."

"I'm merely glad the Tapestry's done." Alison closed her eyes and took a deep breath.

The agent tapped her watch. "Director Winters wants to talk to you."

She opened her eyes. "Okay, have him give me a call."

"We have something better than that." A grin split the woman's face.

A brown-haired man in a dark suit winked into existence beside her. Unlike the bland and forgettable Strands, he sported a handsome face, even though a few wrinkles here and there suggested middle-age had crept up on him. He wasn't her type, but she could easily see a woman, young or otherwise, falling for him.

"I wish I could shake your hand," he said with an apologetic look, "but I'm a hologram, I'm afraid."

"Director Daniel Winters, I presume?" she asked. She knew his name and basic description, but she'd never actually met the man, unlike her parents.

He nodded. "I seem to make a habit of helping Brownstones every few years. Maybe if I'm still around in twenty years, I'll help your kid to fight some aliens or government conspiracy."

Alison grimaced. "I hope my future kid doesn't have to stop weird aliens or government conspiracies." She jabbed a finger in the air at him. "That's your job, isn't it?"

"That it is. That it is. But getting to the point, NOAT and the country owes you a debt, and I'm sorry that just like with your father in LA, no one will ever know what you've really done. They'll think you merely eliminated a group of weird wizards."

"It's okay." She shrugged. "Fame is overrated. But can you at least guarantee me that none of my people will end up in some CIA dungeon somewhere?"

"I'm not the kind of man who throws good people in a hole," Daniel replied. His gaze shifted to Omni. "Or good pets."

Hana frowned. "So you promise you won't try to take him?"

He nodded decisively. "There's no reason to right now, and the last thing we or you want, I suspect, is additional attention. I can't think of a safer place for Omni than with your team. Maybe I'll have someone keep an eye on him every now and again, but if you keep him under control, you'll have no reason to ever see Ophelia or any of my people ever again. Maybe we can coax a few tissue and blood samples out of you?"

"That sounds fair," Hana mumbled. "But no tests for a while. He's been through a lot."

"Understood."

Omni closed his eyes and snuggled into her lap.

"Aww," she whispered. "My little baby's tired after ripping apart the mean old petnapper from another dimension."

Daniel and Ophelia laughed.

"If you or any of your people are ever interested in switching careers," Daniel added, "NOAT would be happy to have you."

"I'll let my team know," Alison responded. "But I'm fine where I am." She smiled at Omni. "But I need to be clear. Is it over? Is the Tapestry really finished? I want to finally give that sigh of relief, you know?"

He nodded. "My people can't find any of the relevant energy signatures other than around Omni. They could be hiding from us somehow like they did before, but we detected any number of powerful signatures once the fight started. We'll pay extra attention to those kinds of indicators for a while, but given what you saw, did, and heard, I think it's reasonable to assume the Tapestry is finished for at least a few years, if not centuries."

She frowned as she considered all her experiences with the aliens. "And now we know magic isn't unique to Earth and Oriceran."

Daniel shook his head. "We don't know that, actually."

"Huh? I sensed magic from those guys. Hana smelled it, too. Even if the Strands themselves weren't magical, the Source can obviously do magic. Probably the Overseer on some level, too."

"But do we know that?" He looked thoughtful for a moment. "It seems more like maybe they tried to reverse-engineer magic and make it work with their strange created bodies. It certainly wasn't magic in the sense of what we see on Earth and Oriceran. From what the Overseer said, it might even be that becoming partially magical was necessary for their kind to survive on Earth."

"But not everyone or everything on Earth is magical," she pointed out.

"For now. Who knows what the centuries will bring? But it doesn't matter anyway."

Alison frowned. "How do you figure?"

"In my line of work, you learn to be happy with the short-term victories. There is always a crisis to bring you down if you let it." Daniel smiled and offered an almost playful shrug.

She laughed. "It's not so different for me."

"Thank you again, Alison. I hope for your sake that we never have to meet again." His image disappeared.

Ophelia extended her hand. "He might not be able to shake your hand, but at least let me do it."

Alison gripped her hand and gave it a firm shake. "You're not bad in a fight. If you ever get bored alien hunting, I could always use someone like you at my company."

"That won't happen. Did you seriously try to swipe a CIA agent out from under the director's nose?"

She shrugged. "It was worth a shot."

CHAPTER TWENTY-NINE

James grunted on the other end of the phone. "This is the kind of shit where you should call and ask for my help. Before, you didn't know, but the minute the government showed up and explained the truth about those fuckers, you should have had me on the phone. I bet the government wouldn't have even minded if I went full Forerunner on those Tapestry assholes. It would have been a fun workout."

Alison had dreaded making this phone call because she assumed her father would respond exactly as he now did. For all of James Brownstone's fine qualities, he was very easy to predict when it came to family matters and chances to deal with people who threatened his little girl.

I'd better nip this is in the bud before he drives up here and throws me in the bed of his truck, tied up for my own protection.

"But we did fine, Dad," she replied and reminded herself that Tahir had secured the phone so they can talk freely. "Between the CIA and Omni, we kicked ass. I'm not saying it wasn't tough, but the important thing is that we won in the end. Any victory you can walk away from is a good one, right?"

"What if Fake Dog didn't change? Where would you be then?" He growled his annoyance. "You could have been killed by the Overseer."

She rolled her eyes even though he couldn't see it. "I simply would have had to work harder. You do remember that among other things, I took on a freaking Mountain Strider, right? That was without your help. And Scott Carlyle in his enchanted power armor. I took him on, too, without your help."

James uttered a long, low, annoyed grunt. "Whispy's gonna be pissed, too. I'm gonna have to hear about it the next time I bond with him. He'll complain and shit. He knows when he's missing out on big fights, and since I don't have as many these days, he bitches and bitches and bitches about it."

"Whispy?" Alison laughed. "Since when do I have to care about what Whispy thinks? He's your symbiont, not mine."

"I'm only saying he might not have been wrong," he mumbled.

"How so?"

"He might have learned something new."

"I doubt it," she replied. "In the end, we destroyed them with good, old-fashioned massive force."

"You said that freak sliced through your shields like nothing near the end." James rumbled ominously, a sure sign of his frustration.

She frowned. "Yeah, so? What does that have to do with

anything? He managed a strike, fine, but I didn't let him get a second hit in."

"Don't you get it? That was a special attack Whispy could have adapted to." Her father muttered something under his breath.

"Yeah," she replied, and sarcasm dripped from her voice. "Because it's so important that you adapt to more things considering you're already probably the single toughest man on Earth."

"You never know," James countered. "It helps to be prepared. Besides, I don't like the CIA. Even if Winters is okay, you never know who might be giving him orders. We've been lucky with people like Senator Johnston, but that could change with one heart attack or stroke when no one's around. Or Winters takes an alien bullet to the head. The next thing you know, we're fighting off CIA agents like I had to before. Your mom had to deal not only with the fucking CIA but all that bullshit with the government hiring freelancers to steal alien shit." He growled.

He's spinning himself up like an overprotective grandma.

Alison sighed. "Maybe I'm the last person who should say this to anyone but, Dad, you worry too much. I'm fine and I'm sorry I didn't call you. I promise that the next time I have to fight weird aliens from another dimension, I'll call you."

"Good. That's all I ask." He fell silent for a few seconds. "And the same shit with me. I shouldn't say this, but maybe you should take a vacation. You have the Tapestry handled and the dark wizards handled. Two of those other princesses are at least kind of your friends. It sounds like a good chance to take some time off."

"I don't know," she admitted. "I've thought about a vacation but at the same time, I'm worried that if I don't settle into a normal routine, it would be bad for my stress."

"Fuck that," James snarled.

"Huh? What the hell, Dad?"

"I'm only saying you're a Brownstone," he pointed out, his voice even deeper than usual. "Because you're a Brownstone, trouble will come looking for you eventually, even if you try to stay out of its way. Trouble might take a detour to visit the Grand Canyon, but it'll always show up in the end. If you have a chance to take a vacation, take it now while trouble's distracted. Get what I'm saying?"

Alison laughed. "That's certainly an elaborate metaphor, but, yeah, I do see what you're saying. I have a wedding to plan, though. I can't plan that if I'm on vacation far away from Seattle. How would I check out venues and that kind of thing?"

James snorted. "The Internet, and according to your mom, you're thinking about not even having a wedding, so what difference does it make?"

Shit. I almost forgot I told her that.

"Nothing's been decided." She let the hesitation creep into her voice. "We might still have some huge event."

"I'm only saying if your plan is to go to the courthouse without a reception, you don't need to waste time on the small details. So go on the damned vacation."

"Okay," she replied. "And to be clear, Dad, as far as the wedding goes, if I do decide on the courthouse, you won't be pissed, will you?"

He took a deep breath and released it slowly. "You need to do what works for you and Mason. I'm not gonna to tell you how to live your life, and I'm not gonna tell you to do shit simply to make me happy. I want you to be happy, and that is more important than making me happy. But, since you asked, if you do have a reception, you should consider barbecue. It doesn't have to be from my place or Jessie Rae's."

"I'll probably not have barbecue," she replied and tried not to laugh. "Maybe some sushi, though."

James grunted. "I take back what I said about you being happy. Sushi at a wedding? That's cruel."

"I don't mind Sonya staying with us but sometimes, it's nice to have the place to ourselves." Alison rested her head on Mason's shoulder and exhaled a contented sigh. She let a frown take over her face. "But I do hope she's having fun at her big drone battle racing event, and that Tahir's not being too much of a dick. I know he means well but sometimes, he gets too much into total mentor mode. She's a talented witch and infomancer, but she's still a teen girl trying to find herself and he doesn't always seem to remember that."

"It'll be fine, A," Mason replied. "Hana's there, and if there is anyone who wants to help Sonya continue to grow out of her shell, it's her. Plus, she can control Tahir easily enough."

"True, but that only reminds me that I'm not so certain about her bringing Omni along."

He shrugged his unoccupied shoulder. "Why? It's not like we have to worry about the Tapestry petnapping him anymore, and the government's made it clear they won't, especially since Hana's willing to give them samples. The only thing Hana, Tahir, and Sonya have to worry about is curious people, and he's easy to explain away as a magical pet. The average person wouldn't even know how unusual he is. They probably think Oriceran's filled with creatures like Omni."

"True enough," she murmured. She let a few long comfortable moments of silence pass before she spoke again. "Just so you know, I'm leaning heavily toward the whole quick wedding and super-long honeymoon deal."

Mason looked at her, a soft smile on his face. "Oh really, now? You sound more like you've decided than you're leaning."

"I don't know about that, but I've talked with both my parents and they're fine with it. Are you sure it won't become a huge problem with your parents?" She looked into his eyes.

He nodded. "It'll be fine, but they'll also be happy if we have a big wedding. But forget about them for now. Let's go back to the discussion of the most important part, the honeymoon. We were so wrapped up in this Tapestry stuff lately, we've barely discussed it."

Alison sighed. "I don't know. I go both ways on it."

"Both ways?" He frowned in confusion. "What do you mean?"

"Part of me thinks it'd be cool to visit Oriceran in a big way," she explained and raised her head from his shoulder. "We could enjoy the kind of wonders you can only find on a planet totally saturated with magic."

"It doesn't sound unappealing. What else were you thinking about?"

Her cheeks heated. "Maybe finding a cabin in the woods away from civilization and camping there for a month. No worries, no phone, no computer, no responsibility. Just you and me. Simple and calm. No wonders and simply endless time together."

A huge grin settled on his face. "I won't complain if you want to spend a month alone with me with no one else distracting you. So I can also say that doesn't sound unappealing, but..." He shrugged.

"But what?" Alison frowned.

"Simple and calm?" He gave her a tight smile. "Let's be real, A. If you really wanted simple and calm, your life and company would be very different. I don't want you to overstress, but I think, on a certain level, you're never truly happy unless there's a lot happening around you."

"Maybe," she mumbled. "I never really thought of it that way. But a wedding's two people. What about you? What do you want?"

"I want to be with you." Mason leaned forward and placed his lips on hers. "That's all I ever wanted."

She half-closed her eyes and surrendered to the kiss, the sudden move pushing out all the lingering concern about future decisions. The Seventh Order was defeated and now, so was the Tapestry. Unlike the last time, no one had to sacrifice their life. It was a total victory, not a Pyrrhic one.

She deepened the kiss, her heart unburdened for the first time in a long time.

I have a man who loves me and friends I care about. I have loving parents, and I help make the world a better place.

I love my life.

Can Alison and her team get a well-deserved break with some downtime or will the bad guys follow them? Find out in <u>DARK REUNION</u>.

Get sneak peeks, exclusive giveaways, behind the scenes content, and more.
PLUS you'll be notified of special **one day only fan pricing** on new releases.

Sign up today to get free stories.

CLICK HERE

or visit: https://marthacarr.com/read-free-stories/

For Hire: Teachers for special school in Virginia countryside.

Must be able to handle teenagers with special abilities.

Cannot be afraid to discipline werewolves, wizards, elves and other assorted hormonal teens.

Apply at the School of Necessary Magic.

AVAILABLE AT AMAZON RETAILERS

Find the compass, save the world or save herself?

Dating is harder for Maggie Parker than running down a felon. Now add in magic.

Did she just see a compass fly?

Can she learn how to use the magic of bubbles to chart a new course in time? It's a lot harder than it sounds.

Join her on her quest to rescue passengers on an ancient ship – a big blue marble called Earth – and save herself.

AVAILABLE ON AMAZON AND IN KINDLE UNLIMITED!

I am easily led astray by other people's ambitions. Just typing that sentence makes me laugh, thank goodness. But, it's still true. I'm going along happily in my lane, my life, enjoying everything that makes it up and then I run smack into a crowd of similar people who are doing it differently. A little trigger goes off in my brain like a marble dropping into a Rube Goldberg machine. It goes around and around without a real point or purpose. (One of my fave artists, by the way)

Last week I was in Scotland at a writer's convention with two hundred other writers, most of them in their thirties and shining with ambition. It was like being with my playmates, so wonderful, so perfect like they were hand selected to hang out with for two whole weeks. I forgot where I was and that it wasn't going to last forever and just stayed in the moment wandering around Edinburgh. I felt like I was back in that college bubble where you really have no idea what's waiting for you out in the so-called real world.

Well, except for one little thing...

There were loads of young writers who were figuring out this business and busting out all over. They had studied all the fine print, all the ways to be a success and applied them and *BANG*, their business was taking off like a rocket. The look of awe on their faces that this thing could actually work was fun to see. How often do we get to celebrate so much of a good thing?

Now, here's the weird part about the committee living in my head and frankly, I think it's similar to a lot of other heads walking around because I'm rarely unique. I'm more general population, middle class no matter what else is happening. If I put on an expensive outfit I'm convinced I'd look like someone from the suburbs who borrowed an expensive outfit.

Anyway, the voices in my head totally ditched how well I'm doing, how perfectly my life is shaping up and started listening for clues that I wasn't doing enough. I was celebrating someone's success while at the same time wondering why I wasn't striving as hard, doing as much, jumping ahead. Day by day at the conference I shrunk inside just a little and panicked a little more. Any of this sound familiar?

None of it was based on reality. Hell, it wasn't even based on what I want in life. It was just that weird trigger that's really old and frankly, a pack of lies. Instead of getting my sense of self from something inward and asking myself first of all, *what do you want*, I was searching for validation based on what others value. Well, based on what I thought others value from what they said. See? Even that is skewed and faulty information.

It also means I've spent waaaaaay too much time thinking about me and not enough being present and just being of service. I forgot one of my hard and fast rules. The universe loves me so stop trying to prove it does. The question has been answered. Get on with things already!

Now I'm back in my nest and I've had a chance to get some sleep and talk with some mentors (who don't encourage my navel gazing) and I'm getting back to my old self. Good news is the whole thing has gotten me to ask, what do I really want? And make some changes so that I get there, instead of someone else's destination. All good news and can lead to more peace and a few fun times. May your road rise up to meet you this week too. More adventures to follow.

THANK YOU for not only reading this story but these *Author Notes* as well.

(I think I've been good with always opening with "thank you." If not, I need to edit the other *Author Notes*!)

RANDOM (*sometimes*) THOUGHTS?

I'm staring at the Eiffel Tower (all lit up, with the light going round at the top like a light-house) and wondering 'how many miles away can people see it?'

No, really.

I'm a few miles away, and it's pretty substantial in my window (I'm on the 10th floor of a hotel.

I know there is a mathematical formula that would tell me (assuming nothing blocks my view), but I'm too lazy to calculate anything.

...

Wait a minute - I wonder what's on the Internet?

Hold on.

Eiffel Tower is 300 m tall (324 to tip), so about 984 ft/1063 ft tall.

And...I failed. I didn't find anything that would allow me to just plug in the numbers and once again, too lazy to figure out arc-cosign or whatever it was in the mathematical formula I just saw.

It was scary. No, seriously. Why do you think I do space opera and not hard sci-fi?

Hard Science Fiction requires math.

At least Urban Fantasy doesn't (usually) require math.

AROUND THE WORLD IN 80 DAYS

One of the interesting (at least to me) aspects of my life is the ability to work from anywhere and at any time. In the future, I hope to re-read my own *Author Notes* and remember my life as a diary entry.

Paris, France

(Yes, I know I'm in Paris, but I just left Switzerland today.)

Zurich is quiet...like creepy quiet.

I was walking to lunch two days ago (a Saturday) from my hotel heading towards a Mexican food restaurant a little over a mile away.

During this walk, I noticed something, and that is the town - a seriously large city, not a tiny little couple of huts in the woods - wasn't making a peep.

I heard the tires of cars driving by, the pedaling of frequent bikes going past...and that is about it. Oh, and I heard a lady talking on her cell phone when she came around the corner.

No birds chirping (seriously - I listened for it.) No children playing. No honking, no music...nothing.

It's seriously odd in my experience.

The next day, we took the train to Lucerne and walked around the tourist area. The sound was back for a while.

I had never realized how much sound I take for granted when I'm in a city. I have family living in small towns, so I expect it when I'm there, but the Swiss in Zurich have this 'shh' effort taken to a new level.

FAN PRICING

$0.99 Saturdays (new LMBPN stuff) and $0.99 Wednesday (both LMBPN books and friends of LMBPN books.) Get great stuff from us and others at tantalizing prices.

Go ahead. I bet you can't read just one.

Sign up here: http://lmbpn.com/email/.

HOW TO MARKET FOR BOOKS YOU LOVE

Review them so others have your thoughts, and tell friends and the dogs of your enemies (because who wants to talk to enemies?). *Enough said ;-)*

Ad Aeternitatem,

Michael Anderle

OTHER BOOKS BY JUDITH BERENS

OTHER BOOKS BY MARTHA CARR

JOIN THE ORICERAN UNIVERSE FAN GROUP ON FACEBOOK!

CONNECT WITH THE AUTHORS

Martha Carr Social

Website: http://www.marthacarr.com

Facebook: https://www.facebook.com/
groups/MarthaCarrFans/

Michael Anderle Social

Michael Anderle Social
Website:
http://www.lmbpn.com

Email List:
http://lmbpn.com/email/

Facebook Here: https://www.
facebook.com/TheKurtherianGambitBooks/

Made in the USA
Middletown, DE
12 December 2021

55301129R00165